DEAD BODY GIRL

judythe morgan

Dead Body Girl

Published by The Danfield Press
Contact: www.judythemorgan.com

Cover Design by Jim Peto
Interior Formatting by Bravia Books

ISBN: 978-1-7365539-8-5
First printing

Published in the United States of America.

For Ambassador James Nolan and his wife, Mary-Dee, who many years ago encouraged me to write a story about the dead body found on the riverbank of the Shenandoah River below their home. Their ideas and help with the plotting and shared research shaped Dead Body Girl into the story you are about to read.

Thank you, Jim and Mary-D. You'll read it in Heaven, but I did write the story for you like I promised. Finally.

CHAPTER ONE

EARLY MORNING DEW sparkled in the rising sun of the April day. The ribbon of roadway wound through the soft foothills of northeast Virginia, twisting along with the Shenandoah River threading through the area. Not cool enough for the heater, yet too cool for the AC. Scents of spring whipped inside the lowered car windows.

Anticipation filled Mary-Dee Ross.

Sometimes these farm sales were Aladdin's cave filled with treasures, other times a trash dump. Either way, estate sales were the lifeblood of her antiques business. Not that she hadn't tried all the other means. Estate sales were a much faster way to get merchandise than sitting through auctions waiting for the one thing she wanted, only to be outbid. Buying pre-filled containers from Europe had proven too expensive for what she received. So many of the things delivered were charity shop items, not true antiques. She wasn't doing that again.

She approached the farmhouse where dozens of cars were parked at various angles in the yard and field. Wishing she'd spent a little less time over her morning tea, she guided her SUV off the road and hopped out.

With her lucky straw hat on her head and comfortable muck boots on her feet, she powerwalked to the clapboard house. Not once had she regretted her decision to leave the FBI and pursue this life.

People wandered through the assortment of items spread around the yard. Some trailed inside the barn and others up the porch stairs into the house. The front porch overflowed with furniture—oak sofa tables, enamel-top kitchen tables, marble tops, pie safes, china cabinets, and dozens of assorted chairs.

Around the corner, on the side porch, she spotted a Hoosier cabinet. One of her clients was looking for a vintage baking center. Mary-Dee tucked her elbows close and scooted between furniture and people to examine the piece. She opened a cabinet door to peek inside. Someone shoved from the other direction. "Excuse me. You're blocking the aisle."

"Sorry." Mary-Dee swung the door closed and stared into the face of Meena Nolan. A lump the size of Mount Vernon filled her throat, blocking her air and stealing the moisture from her mouth. "Meena? I mean, Ms. Nolan?"

"Mary-Dee." The flabby skin hanging below the elderly woman's biceps swayed. She scooped Mary-Dee into a "Meena" hug. Grey hair stiff from AquaNet scratched Mary-Dee's cheek, and the familiar scent of Hermes Caleche filled her nostrils. The woman bought every bottle of the sixties vintage scent Mary-Dee found when she'd been one of her best customers. She'd missed Meena Nolan. Her hugs and her perfume. Not the stiff hair.

"Let's find someplace where we can catch up." Meena slipped her arm through Mary-Dee's. Before she could politely refuse, Meena guided her off the porch toward a group of wrought iron chairs beneath a sprawling sweetgum tree. Meena settled onto the loveseat and pointed Mary-Dee to one of the matching chairs.

"I'm not sure we should be sitting on these. Sellers don't like it when you mess with their stuff."

Meena's hands flapped in dismissal. "It's okay. I've bought it. So, sit. Tell me how you've been."

Mary-Dee's head spun like a merry-go-round. She made an arch in the grass with the toe of her boot. What had changed? Meena hadn't spoken to her in over a year. Now this, like old times. Didn't make sense.

"I'm good. I'd love to visit, but I need to check out that Hoosier. I have a client who wants one." She pushed to her feet.

"Sit. Darlene wants too much for it. It's not going anywhere."

"This is Darlene's estate sale? I had no idea."

"I tried to tell her she should contact an estate liquidator to run it for her. Now that she sees this madhouse, I bet she wishes she had."

"Have her call me. I'll work with her on whatever's left." Mary-Dee started to stand again. "I should go check out that Hoosier."

"Keep your pants on." Meena pulled her phone from her purse. "Darlene, it's Meena. I want the Hoosier too. Okay. Thanks." She smiled at Mary-Dee and slid her phone back into her purse. "Done."

"But what if my client doesn't want it?"

"No problem. I'll consign it to you, and you'll sell it. Enough about that. What's been going on with you?"

Mary-Dee fidgeted, unsure of the why behind Meena's renewed interest. "Business slowed after … you know … it's building again."

Meena's shoulders dipped in a heavy sigh. "Gus tells me all the time I shouldn't have blamed you. I'm sorry."

Mary-Dee's hands went cold. "Gus is here?"

Meena's gaze shifted over Mary-Dee's shoulder. "See for yourself."

She took a deep breath and turned.

Slow and easy, Gus Nolan strolled toward them. His shoulders relaxed, his steps confident. Streaks of grey peppered his sideburns, but his body was still six-foot of toned muscle. He didn't make eye contact, yet the hairs on her arm rose.

"Mary-Dee." He tipped his head her way and sat beside his grandmother. His eyes, the color of black tea, settled on her. "How're you doing?"

She bit her bottom lip and shoved a sweetgum ball sticker into the soft dirt, burying its prickly exterior. His tone was formal, not harsh, more disinterested. An interrogation voice like Todd used with witnesses whenever he called her to the station to sketch a suspect.

"Fine. Just fine." She matched his tone. Leaning forward, she took Meena's hand into hers and softened her voice. "I need to get back to looking before all the best stuff is gone. Nice seeing you. I hope to see you in the shop again soon."

Meena cast a sideways glance at Gus. With a generous smile, she patted Mary-Dee's hand. "Count on it, honey."

A new page turned in her relationship history with Meena Nolan. She'd missed Meena and seeing her friend felt like a new beginning.

But Gus? She wasn't so sure. Why on earth was he back in Mount Pleasant? Hadn't he already messed up her life enough?

———

Gus gave Mary-Dee's retreat a long steady survey. He saw pieces of the girl he'd known and loved. Her auburn hair poked out from under her lucky hat. Longer now than before, but other than that, she didn't look a day older than she had when she'd joined him and Claudia at Quantico. At the same time, she was different, changed. Surer of herself. He saw a cold fire in her hazel eyes, heard it in her voice. An attitude that said, I won't be gullible again.

They'd been friends, pals, heading for something more until his undercover assignment with her sister. An assignment that had gone south, and he hadn't been able to save Claudia or find who'd killed her. Yet. And for that, he'd never forget or forgive himself.

Neither would Mary-Dee.

"Gus! Are you listening?" His grandmother Meena's voice penetrated his thoughts. "For goodness' sake, your brain's been a mess since you got back. Pay attention."

"I was. You want this iron yard set loaded. Then … hmm, okay, maybe I drifted off. Show me what else goes in the truck."

Mary-Dee had always messed with his head. This wasn't any different. He didn't want to screw up her world again, but rejecting this undercover assignment after he'd blotched the last one had not been a choice.

More like karmic punishment.

His whole career teetered with Mary-Dee at the center. He had to bring the smuggler down and keep her safe. Cases like this could, no *would*, be punctuated with moments of terrifying violence.

Violence was the very thing that drove Mary-Dee to resign from the Agency, now it lurked at her doorstep. He wouldn't fail this time.

Mary-Dee slid into the parking space beside her shop in the small strip center on Route 50. When the retail space became available, she'd jumped at the chance to sign a lease and move out of her spaces in an antique mall miles away.

Kayley held the shop door open for her. Her wavy black-brown hair haloed her Mayan princess face and cascaded over her shoulder. Dark ebony eyes danced in the sunlight and her smile lifted her broad cheekbones. She nodded toward the overflowing box of things from the estate sale. "Looks like you had a bumper-crop run."

"Wait till you see. There's more in the car. I had to lower the backseat." Mary-Dee carried the overflowing box to the sales counter.

Kayley followed with another box. One by one Mary-Dee lined items on the 1900s feedstore counter that served for checkout. "And I also found a Hoosier I think the Crawfords will love. It's being delivered."

"An excellent run indeed. See any dealers you knew?"

"Just about everyone. The place was packed." She lifted a Tiffany-style lamp onto the counter.

"Meena was there. Turns out it was her sister-in-law's sale."

Kayley's hand stilled. "Darlene's, really? And?"

"We talked a bit."

"About time you two ended the silliness."

Mary-Dee nodded. "Gus was there, too."

"Ahh. How'd that go?"

"Well, he didn't stab me, and I didn't stab him."

"That *is* progress." Kayley winked.

Gus pulled his truck next to Meena's ancient Lincoln Town Car in their shared driveway. With the trunk opened, there was almost as much stuff inside the cavern-like space as the bed of his pickup.

With her arms loaded, Meena headed into the house. "I'll be right back. That stuff goes in the barn storage side for now and make sure the yard set is where you can get to it," she called. "My book club's coming up and I'm planning a garden setting. I want it cleaned and ready for that."

"I'll take care of the garden set first."

Her book club was the highlight of Meena's world. She loved playing hostess and anything she planned was always a major social event for Mount Pleasant. There wasn't much else for entertainment in the rural Virginia town.

"Come along for a cup of tea when you finish unloading."

He reversed his truck and pulled around to the large barn. The entire front half of the forty-by-seventy structure housed her *treasures*. Vintage furniture filled the large floor space. Shelves full of smalls lined the walls. Everything from salt cups to epergnes and Confederate relics from the days when the area housed a Confederate hospital.

When he'd gone off to college, she'd converted the back section into a barndominium apartment for him. A perfect arrangement then and now, close enough to watch out for the grandmother who raised him yet gives him his privacy.

He lifted one of the wrought iron chairs off the truck bed and put it beside the barn door. Twenty minutes later, he sat across from his grandmother at a small table on the screened porch that surrounded three sides of the 1800s farmhouse.

"You do know eventually you're going to run out of space for stuff out there and in here," he said.

He loved the rich laugh that shook her shoulders.

"Nah, there's always room for one more trinket or piece of furniture. I did well at Darlene's this morning."

"Plus, you reconnected with Mary-Dee like I asked."

Detective Harrison would not be happy that Gus had jumped the gun and seen Mary-Dee before their scheduled meeting with her. Gus couldn't help himself. He wasn't comfortable with their first encounter being her, learning the reason he was back was to be her bodyguard.

Crow's feet formed in the corners of Meena's eyes as she smiled. "It was time. Past time. I love that girl. I've missed her."

"You shouldn't have been angry with her in the first place. I'm over it—water under the bridge."

"It'll be interesting to see how it goes when you deliver the Hoosier to her shop. Did you know she's still doing those suspect sketches?"

"Really?" he countered evasively. He'd been briefed on Mary-Dee when his boss, Eric made the assignment.

"I don't like it. A while back some battered girl ran into her shop. Mary-Dee did the sketch that caught the guy. Turned out he was some hot-shot gangster from DC. She convinced the girl to testify and go into witness protection. Wait, the trial's coming up …"

Her eyebrows dipped low. "Is that why you've come back—that missing girl?"

The missing witness offered a convenient cover for the real reason he'd returned. He couldn't acknowledge that to his grandmother or Mary-Dee though. Only Todd Harrison, his pal from their Agency days, now Chief of Detectives for Mount Pleasant, knew the smuggling issue was the real reason Gus returned.

No one else needed to know. Certainly not Mary-Dee.

"I told you. I'm on a break. But I agree, those guys are nothing to mess with. If Todd needs me, I'll watch out for her."

"Break? You never take time off. Kinda sounds like you mighta been fired."

"I haven't been fired." *Not yet anyway.* "Agents do get time off, you know."

He couldn't blow this undercover assignment. Or he might be fired.

His boss had been sympathetic since Gus'd nearly died himself, but he mishandled his last assignment, and the head of the international smuggling operation got away. Eric had not been sympathetic about that.

He pushed from the table. "Think I'll start on the yard set. Not that long till your book club meeting."

CHAPTER TWO

"I'M GOING TO clean and price these things so we can get them out quickly. Will you watch up here?" Mary-Dee asked Kayley.

"Of course," her assistant answered with a smile.

Mary-Dee picked up a box of things from the farm sale and headed to the kitchen area. A few minutes later, the bell on the shop door jingled.

Not the jolting buzz sound of an electronic door alarm like Todd wanted her to install, but the soft chime of an antique bell suspended on a coiled strip of copper. She'd picked up the bell on a buying trip in England to use in her shop. She peeked around the bookshelves separating the small kitchenette in the back from the display area. Gus came in with Darlene's son Butch.

Whatever they wanted Kayley would manage. Mary-Dee concentrated on the dirt around the handle of the ironstone pitcher, tipped the pitcher to rinse, set it aside, and submerged another ironstone bowl in the tepid water.

She sensed Gus's presence behind her before he spoke. She'd never been able to erase the outdoorsy scent he used.

"We brought the Hoosier. Kayley said you'd tell us where you want it."

Her elbow bumped into his chest when she turned. She stood momentarily paralyzed by the stir of familiarity the touch produced. Water from her hands dribbled on his shoes.

Gus, looking totally unaffected, shook the droplets off his shoe, reached around her for the towel on the counter, and handed it to her.

She dried her hands, determined not to show any further reaction. "Okay. There's space in the layaway room. Put it there until the Crawfords can come look at it. Glad Butch could help you."

"Me, too." He moved aside. "He's strong. Wrestling team in high school, remember? His being Downs never stopped him."

"Right. He's my go-to when I need muscle."

Walking ahead, she led Gus to the storage/layaway room. Together they shoved a couple of other pieces aside to make room.

She admired the Hoosier after Butch and Gus moved it into the space. "It's so rare to find one with original hardware and glass. If my client doesn't want it, it'll sell quickly."

"Aunt Meena's problem now. It's off our porch. Pop said he was suffocating with all the stuff. Mama had to get rid of some of it, or he was going to have the biggest bonfire in the county." Butch chuckled. "He meant it too."

"Your dad needs to tell his sister the same thing. The barn-dominium is about to explode, the house is bursting at the seams, and Meena keeps buying more stuff," Gus said.

"Antiques can be addictive. It's what keeps me in business."

Her phone rang. She glanced at the screen. Todd Harrison, Mount Pleasant Police. He must need another suspect sketch done.

"Sorry, I have to take this." She stepped away. "Hi, Todd. Give me a minute. I'll call you right back, okay?"

"Still working with him?" Gus asked when she returned.

Like Meena, Gus wasn't happy with her sketch work or her ongoing relationship with their high school friend.

Nodding, she walked with Gus and Butch to the truck. "Thanks for the help."

"You're very welcome." Gus looked like he was going to say something else. Instead, he pressed his lips together and climbed into the truck.

Watching the truck disappear down the road, Mary-Dee dismissed the strange feeling circling her body and returned Todd's call. "What's up?"

"I've got something to share with you, just not over the phone." His voice sounded mysterious.

"Okay. Sure. I'll be right down."

Once back inside, she said, "Todd called. I've got to run into town. I'll be back as soon as I can."

Kayley gave a thumbs up. "Gotcha ya covered."

―――――――――

Mary-Dee waved to the desk sergeant on her way to Todd's office in the open pit area where officers worked. Always reminded her of a beehive. Sarge was on the phone and signaled her to wait for a minute.

She sat in a wooden chair along the wall. Every time she returned to the station, she wondered if the young girl she'd helped, Gianna, was okay in her new life.

What happened that day would always haunt her.

A car had skidded to a stop in front of her shop, sending pings of gravel against the display window. Gianna stumbled out and ran inside. The midday sun flashed through the open door.

"Can I use your phone?" The girl glanced over her shoulder at the highway.

Her knees were bloody, her face bruised, and her dress torn. Her eyes shifted back and forth to the picture windows at the front of the store. "Hurry, please."

Dropping her feathered duster, Mary-Dee pulled her phone from her apron pocket. Her hand shook. "Here."

Gianna grabbed the phone and moved behind a large armoire.

Mary-Dee quickly wrote the license plate number of the older model car with its crushed trunk and shattered passenger side windshield on her palm. She strained to hear the girl's conversation but couldn't make out every word. Something about being found out, needing a place to go.

"Okay." Gianna shoved the phone at her and turned toward the door.

Mary-Dee gripped her arm. "Wait. Let me help. You need to see a doctor. I can call someone."

"No. I'm fine. And you can't tell anyone I was here. Please."

Too worried for her, Mary-Dee had called Todd. She liked to think because she had alerted him, Gianna was now secure in a safe house and her testimony would put her abuser behind bars for a long, long time.

Todd opened the door to his glassed-off office bringing her back to the present moment and motioned her inside. "Sorry to keep you waiting."

"No worries. How can I help?" She patted her art supply case. "I'm ready."

"I should've said you wouldn't need that today. Have a seat."

Mary-Dee ran her tongue along the inside of her pursed lips. That didn't sound good. "Is this about Gianna? I read where the trial's coming up."

"It is." He settled into his squeaky desk chair. "She's disappeared."

"From the safe house? How is that possible?"

"I don't like to admit it, but it happens often. Her handler believes she's gone to see her family. She kept talking about how much she missed them. We checked. She didn't. They promised to contact us if she shows up, but Gianna has so far managed to evade our efforts to track her. We're thinking she might try to contact you."

"Why would she do that?"

"You two connected while you worked on those sketches. You're the one who convinced her to testify and go into WITSEC. I'm not saying she will contact you, but if she does, I want you to be ready. And call me."

"Of course."

"On a different topic, have you had any trouble since the break-in last month?"

"It was not a break-in. We accidently left the back door unlocked. Kayley shouldn't have wasted your time. Some kid needing a quick buck to buy his next hit or a place to crash overnight pushed it open. He must have been disappointed when he saw all the old stuff. He won't be back."

"All the same. With Gianna missing, MS-13 will have someone watching your shop closely. Her testimony will send their gang member to jail for a long time. They'll do whatever it takes to protect their own."

His eyes met hers. "Keep your phone handy. You see someone or something out of the ordinary—anything—call me."

Defiance raised her shoulders. "I'm quite capable of taking care of myself." She might have left the FBI, but she hadn't forgotten her training and kept up, jogging and target practice regularly.

His concerned gaze morphed into a frown. "DO NOT cop an attitude with me. This is serious. These people don't mess around, and they're looking for her. That puts you in the bullseye. Be careful."

"Fine. Is this little lecture why you called me in?"

"Not completely. I wanted to let you know finding Gianna is a joint effort, Feds and local. The FBI is sending an agent—."

His office door flew open, and Gus waltzed in. "Sorry, I'm late."

Her eyebrow quirked up. "Gus? Gus is the agent?" Her voice shook in disbelief.

Gus dragged the extra chair beside her. Close. Too close. She could smell the all-too-familiar spicey aftershave, Wild Country. Their first Christmas she'd given him a bottle.

"Yes." Todd's eyes met hers. "He'll be working with you at the shop. Keeping an eye out."

"No. I do not need a bodyguard."

"The bureau thinks otherwise. They're calling the shots on this one," Todd replied. "And the plan works. He's an old family friend home on leave, helping out."

Angling his head with a cockiness that glinted from his eyes, Gus grinned. "Gonna be like old times. The three of us working together."

She snarked a half laugh and squeezed her art satchel to her chest. "And we all know how those ended."

Detention, suspension. Grounding.

The glint in Gus's eyes dulled. He remembered too, and his memories weren't any happier than hers.

Mary-Dee shifted her focus to Todd. "You can't be serious."

Todd's neck muscles bulged. His jaw went taut. He morphed into the stern detective persona convincing a witness how necessary their cooperation was. "Deadly serious. MS-13 gang members have been on the most wanted list for years and will always be a real threat. You have no choice. Forget about the past. Focus on now."

Gus squirmed. "Todd's right. These guys play tough, and it isn't always pretty."

"I understand. Gianna's stories were frightening. But I don't need protection." *Especially not from someone who got my sister killed.* "You forget I trained as an agent. I'd rather take care of myself."

"It's not an option." Todd leaned forward with his elbows on the desktop. "You bowed out of field work. Gus will be there."

"But—"

"No buts. He starts tomorrow."

"Hmm ... about that, I kinda started today. Butch and I delivered a ..." He turned to her. "What'd you call that thing?"

"A Hoosier," she spit the word out.

"I also noticed you're gonna need to do some security camera upgrades around the building."

"But Todd installed new equipment and there are already cameras in the parking area and on the corners of the other buildings. The intersection even has red-light cameras. Why more? My budget's stretched tight."

"It'll be covered." Todd pushed from his desk. "Gus and I need to sort some paperwork and details. You're free to go. I'll walk you to your car."

———

Gus waited while Todd escorted Mary-Dee out. Waiting was, after all, a major part of his job—stakeouts, briefings, hearings, postmortems. He'd learned to wait well.

Early in their law enforcement careers, he and Todd had been partners. Todd found his niche in their small-town police force and local county politics. Gus preferred more action and the worldwide scope of the FBI.

Yet here he was, back in his hometown where it all began, and uncertain about exactly what that was going to mean.

Todd returned. A smug smile tipped his cheeks upward. "Feelings still there I see."

Lifting his shoulders, Gus refused to squirm. "No way."

Todd shook his head slowly like a pendulum winding down and slid behind his desk. "You're still blind where she's concerned. You ought to admit it, at least to yourself."

Tension ran like a red-hot wire through the room.

Gus ground his back teeth. He wasn't arguing relationships. Past or present. "Shall we get on with business?"

He reached down to retrieve his laptop, flipped it open, and pointed to the large screen on the wall to Todd's left.

"There's been a rash of thefts in Europe."

So what? flashed in Todd's eyes. His brow rose, but he said nothing.

Gus continued, "Important thefts, mainly from museums but also individual collections in France, Spain, Italy, and England. Gems, coins, stamps, and the like. It's believed the stolen articles are smuggled into the States inside antique containers. The goods are hidden in a piece, then exported, retrieved, and ultimately disposed of. Leads point to local, well-respected antique shops and small-time auction houses. Several possibilities in this area and the agency wants an operative inside."

Todd interrupted him. "Mary-Dee's shop? Can't be."

"All I know is I saw an English 1800s walnut stationery box from the stolen objects list in her shop this morning when Butch and I made that delivery. I'll verify when I go tomorrow."

"And you think she's in on it?"

"At this point, we're not saying she knows anything about the illegal use of her shop, but the evidence is strong her place is being used."

"I don't believe she's involved."

"I don't want to," Gus agreed. "But facts are facts. The trail leads to her shop. Either Mary-Dee or someone at her shop is working with the smugglers."

"Why not just ask her?"

"We have no concrete evidence. Yet." He paused. "It's

generally believed Mary-Dee knows nothing of the illegal use of her shop. Her answer wouldn't matter either way. She's not who we're after. Nailing the head of the smuggling gang is our goal. He, or she, is clever, slippery. We want him … or her … stopped. You said you'd seen an uptick in break-ins around here where it appears nothing was taken. That fits the pattern we're seeing from D.C. and further south. Didn't her shop have a break-in?"

Todd frowned. "That doesn't make her guilty."

"Right, and ignorance won't protect her if things go south. Her shop is involved. The Bureau's closing in on the operation. MS-13's watching her. That trial is fast approaching. The next few weeks could bring the whole thing down around her. She needs discreet protection from someone trained in these situations, who can handle smugglers and gang members. Someone who can stay close without creating speculation like you just explained to her."

"I was referring to our missing witness situation. Not the smuggling."

"True and no one counted on the missing witness twist to double the importance of having me there. Plus, it supplies the perfect cover for the real reason Mary-Dee can never know."

"I don't like not telling her the whole story."

"You think I do?" Glaring at Todd, Gus shoved out of his chair, paced wall to wall in the small office, rubbing the back of his neck. Secrets and promises never worked out.

"It's the worst part of what we do. But it's our job." Gus slammed his computer shut. "If we end up bringing your MS-13 guy down *and* this smuggling ring all the better. Two for one. What do you have on the missing girl?"

Todd opened his laptop and projected a file on the screen. "Not near what you have on the smuggling."

"Giddy up, partner. Together we'll figure it out."

CHAPTER THREE

MARY-DEE WATCHED TODD disappear through the Police Department's front door and dug her cell from her purse. Her hand shook. She tightened her grip. "Kayley, how's it going?"

"Great. That couple came to look at the Hoosier and loved it. We'll need to deliver."

"The Crawfords. Wonderful. I'll get Butch to help. Could you close for me tonight?"

"Sure. Everything okay? You sound a little stressed. Tough sketch session?"

"It's not that. We'll talk tomorrow. Thanks. I owe you."

Until Mary-Dee met Kayley at an auction, she'd run the shop alone and closed whenever she had to leave to do a sketch. Some of which could be miles away. Hanging a sign saying she'd "be back soon" every time she left did not bring return customers or build confidence in shoppers. Meena helped when she could, but that came to a halt when Gus dumped her for Claudia.

Mary-Dee kept crossing paths with Kayley at estate sales and auctions. They soon became friends, and she'd hired her part-time. Kayley turned out to be quick with figures, tireless with details, and the biggest bonus being, she knew antiques. Mary-Dee'd put her on full-time and had come to depend on her for occasions like today when she needed time alone.

Confident the shop was in good hands, she headed to the one place that had always been her Superman Fortress of Solace, her secret sanctuary. The place where she recharged whenever her world did a tilt-a-whirl. Today she truly needed a rest from the Kryptonite of Gus Nolan being back in her life.

Traffic made the drive from downtown take nearly an hour. She slowed her speed when she spotted the turn off the main highway to the covered bridge and her private spot. The Nolan family farm was down the two-lane road, upriver on the banks of the Shenandoah. She and Claudia had ridden their bikes over this same bridge dozens of times, hoping to spot Gus on his way to his grandmother's.

In summers, the three of them carried giant inner tubes down the stairs in Meena's backyard to the river. They rode the tubes downriver and went swimming in the deep waters beside the bridge. Challenging one another to see who could swing the farthest off the rope Gus tied from the huge oak tree on the bank. Other memories surfaced. She squeezed the steering wheel until blue veins popped in her hand like an old woman's.

Nope. Not going there.

She eased off the accelerator to make the turn and let the rhythmic clickety-clack of her tires over the wooden planks refocus her errant thoughts. With her SUV secured off the narrow road, she grabbed a blanket from the backseat, climbed down the bank, and sat with her back against the tree. Her focus settled on the ripples of the flowing river.

In the clear water at the edges, she could see the sandy bottom and recalled the feel of mud between her toes, the sounds of splashing water, and her sister's laughter played in her head. Her throat heated with tears. She swallowed, refocusing on the gentle waves rippling in the deep, dark middle where light sparked on the surface. Her life had gone dark for so long after she lost Claudia.

She quit the FBI and moved home to Mount Pleasant. Not one to wander aimlessly, she'd taken business classes at the local college and opened her antique shop. Antiques were in her blood, after all. She inherited her aunt's inventory when she passed away and started small. It hadn't been easy to find inner peace again, but MDR Antiques gave her focus. Working with Todd on suspect sketches for their hometown police kept her Bureau training active. The best of both worlds.

She'd been sure she'd laid the past to rest, and finally found her happy place again. Her resentment of Gus and his part in what happened had taken a bit longer to unleash, but she believed she'd let go of that too. Her shoulders caved.

Until today.

She leaned her head back against the tree trunk and closed her eyes, willing the anger roaring in her head to stop.

Thirty minutes later, a voice pierced her sleepy solitude. She forced her eyes open. The very image in her head that she wanted to forget stood in front of her.

"Mary-Dee?" Gus's gaze searched hers. "What are you doing here?"

Her pulse stuttered a bit. "I could ask you the same question."

"It's my jogging route, don't you remember?"

"I've never seen you."

"And I've never seen you, which leads back to my original question. What are you doing here?" he asked again.

"I come here for peace and quiet. To be alone."

"Did it ever occur to you this spot is a little too isolated considering the FBI's most wanted gang is watching you?"

Standing in the setting sun, his shoulders glimmered with perspiration from his run. His dark hair thick and untidy. His mouth arrogantly curved. He was so outrageously

good-looking, and he knew it. That alone made him positive-
ly infuriating.

Always had.

"You're forgetting I trained at the Bureau. I know how to
handle myself."

"I haven't forgotten, but you settled for a desk job after …"
His voice went soft, trailed off.

He didn't have to say the words. They both knew why she'd
chosen the path she took.

"I didn't settle. I chose to leave. My art skills have helped
Todd and so many others do their job. I wasn't cut out for
what you and Claudia did. If she'd listened to me and gotten
out too, she might still be alive."

"Don't you think I regret what happened every day of my
life? I will never forget. Or forgive myself for how it happened."

Mary-Dee shoved to her feet and started past him. He
stepped into her path, blocked her, and rested his hand on her
forearm. "If you're worried I'll screw up this time, don't. I'm
not the flippant young agent I was then. Please don't come
here again unless you tell me or Todd where you're going."

"I will not let this situation, or you, control my life." She
jerked her arm from his grip and stomped to her SUV.

Gus clenched his fists, clamping his molars until he was sure
he'd cracked his already crowned tooth. This stubborn streak
in Mary-Dee was something new, and he didn't like it. Claudia
had been the hardheaded, daredevil sister pulling Mary-Dee
along on her coattails. Claudia paid the price for her reckless-
ness. Things might have turned out so differently if Claudia
had only listened to him.

She hadn't and lost her life. He wasn't going to let that Ross
stubbornness cause him to lose Mary-Dee.

He made his way up to the road and sprinted the last of his run to burn away the frustration.

And guilt.

The next day, Gus arrived at MDR Antiques before Mary-Dee. He sipped his coffee and waited. Her SUV pulled into the parking lot, and he stepped out of his truck to meet her at the shop entrance.

"Good morning." He reached to take the box she carried.

"I got it." She shifted the cardboard container onto her hip and unlocked the shop door. "How long have you been out there?"

"A while."

She exhaled a noisy huff. "Don't come early again. I don't want the other shopping center tenants to think I'm under surveillance or that they are. Worse yet, call the police to arrest you for stalking. It's bad enough Todd has patrol cars buzzing by regularly. I'll get you a key."

"Whatever you want, boss." Perfect, now he'd be able to snoop without her around.

She set the box on the counter and pivoted to stare into the chest hairs peeking from the vee of his shirt. His breath blew on the top of her head. She flat-palmed her hand against his chest and pushed him back. "I don't like any of this. I think it's all unnecessary, but I have no choice so I'll do the best I can to co-operate. Just stay out of my way. No talk of the past. You're the agent assigned until after the trial. That's it."

"As you wish, boss." He swept his hand low and dipped his knee in a princely bow.

The shop bell jingled, and Kayley walked in. "Oh my. Another fair prince already swept away by milady I see."

"He's no fair prince, but he will be hanging around until Gia—"

Gus flashed a scowl with a barely perceptible headshake. "Until her majesty kicks me out ... or banishes me."

Kayley clutched her sides with a loud belly laugh. "I can't wait to watch this show."

"Enough already." Mary-Dee filled the vintage cashbox from the bank envelope.

"What's on the docket for today, boss lady?" Kayley asked.

"Let's finish cleaning the standing cases. I'll polish the furniture pieces."

"On it." Kayley headed to the kitchen area.

"I'll help Kayley." Gus followed her to the supply bin. She handed him a bottle of blue liquid for the glass and a roll of paper towels along with a squirt bottle of tepid water and soft rags.

"For the smalls, that's glassware like plates and figurines, tchotchkes. Can't use commercial glass cleaner on them. Too harsh." She wound a path through the furniture to the glass cases stretching floor to ceiling on the far wall.

Staying out of Mary-Dee's way, Gus noted her routine and studied the shop layout. Kayley offered Cliff's Notes descriptions of the smalls. He didn't have the heart to tell her growing up with his grandmother he probably knew as much or more than she did.

While they dusted and cleaned, Mary-Dee greeted customers and showed pieces, explaining the background, and dickering over prices. Gus was impressed. She'd made the transition from FBI agent to antique shop entrepreneur smoothly. Her people skills made her a successful sketch artist and now owner of a profitable business, if the discreet price tags he'd seen were any indication.

So why, then, would she risk her business by being involved with smuggling? Was it possible she wasn't aware of the operation going on under her nose?

Kayley arranged the smalls on the now shiny glass shelf.

Mary-Dee's assistant's file had been sketchy, but not criminal. A couple of citations for selling reproduction antiques as real never amounted to jail time. Warnings and fines, but it could have led to smuggling for bigger profits.

Was she the smuggler's insider? Possibly.

Being Mary-Dee's right hand would make it easy for her to pass along stolen objects, but Gus saw no motive. That didn't mean there weren't any.

"Earth to Gus." Kayley's voice penetrated his thoughts. "Lunchtime."

"I didn't bring lunch. I'll need to grab something."

"I'd be happy to share." Kayley offered an inviting smile.

"Perhaps another time," Mary-Dee said, a frown on her face. "I need his help to deliver the Hoosier to the Crawford's house. Gus, okay to use your truck? Butch's is in the shop. Darlene is dropping him off. On the way back, Meena wants us to stop by. She has a Victorian etagere and some other pieces she wants us to pick up for consignment."

"About time she got rid of some stuff. The house is bursting at the seams, and you can hardly walk through the barn," he said.

Kayley crossed her arms. "I think she saw how quickly the Hoosier sold and is ready to cash in. Your grandmother is a shrewd operator."

Gus juggled Kayley's comment in his head. His forehead wrinkled. Interesting. He'd never considered his Meena shrewd. But then he'd never thought Mary-Dee could be involve with a smuggling operation either. Maybe his bosses were right, he was losing his edge.

CHAPTER FOUR

"I CALL SHOTGUN," Butch shouted after they'd loaded the Hoosier into the bed of Gus's 1976 pickup. With a toothy grin aimed at Gus, Butch held the passenger door open for Mary-Dee.

Shooting him a killer scowl she stepped on the running board then slid across the bench seat, wishing the floor-mounted stick shift offered more of a barrier between her and Gus.

He climbed behind the wheel. His elbow brushed Mary-Dee's forearm when he started the engine and shifted into gear. His eyes apologized when they met hers.

She tucked her arm closer and inched toward Butch careful not to rub thighs on either side.

"Can one of you navigate?" Gus asked.

Mary-Dee flapped a slip of paper. "Mrs. Crawford gave me directions They're simple. US 50 to 81 to 703 to Spruce Hollow Road."

"I'd still like a GPS route up."

"Have you forgotten your way around?" she accused.

"No. Just prefer having backup."

Butch dug his cell from the bib of his coveralls. "I can do that."

"Thanks." Gus guided the truck up the highway entrance ramp. The truck didn't have air conditioning, and the lovely spring weather of two weeks ago had vanished into a summer-like day. Warm air blew strands of hair across Mary-Dee's face. They shouted to be heard, and conversation dwindled to the whistle of wind through the windows.

"Right. Coming up," Butch said.

Gus slowed, watching for a turn.

Mr. and Mrs. Crawfords' home sat at the end of a country lane with soybean fields on either side. With its high-pitched gable roof and dormer windows, the Victorian farmhouse was picture-perfect. Mrs. Crawford motioned them around the house where her husband directed Gus to a rear porch with the screen door propped open.

Gus backed the truck to a stop as close as he could. Butch and Mr. Crawford carried the base while she and Gus followed with the lighter top.

"Are you sure you should be lifting this? It's kinda heavy. Butch and I can get it."

She peeked around the cabinet top. "Who do you think helped Butch before you showed up?"

"Right. Sorry. No offense meant."

Minutes later, Mrs. Crawford clasped her hands to her cheek. "It's like it was always meant to be there."

Everything about the Crawford home reminded Mary-Dee of her Aunt Nellie's. After her dad died, her mom loaded up Mary-Dee and her sister to return to Mount Pleasant to live in the enormous Victorian that had been their family home for generations. If it hadn't been for Aunt Nellie, she and her sister would have been foster care statistics when her mother slipped into depression and took her life.

Instead of rules about what she and Claudia could and

couldn't touch in the home filled with antiques and precious heirlooms, Aunt Nellie told them fabulous stories about each antique piece. Back then Mary-Dee and her sister didn't appreciate the *old* stuff. As each of them finished high school they left, Claudia first, off to interview with the FBI after spotting an employment posting in the Post Office. Mary Dee to art school and then the Bureau.

Claudia craved the adventure, the excitement, the danger she found as an agent. For Mary-Dee, being with Gus was the appeal. Claudia excelled with undercover assignments, especially when partnered with Gus. Lying did not set well with Mary-Dee even though she knew it was a necessary part of undercover work. The way they caught the bad guys.

Only she'd never been a good liar. Claudia, on the other hand, had no problem with stretching and bending the truth in her job or life.

Mary-Dee shook off the threatening wave of sadness and extended her hand to both Crawfords. "It is the perfect addition. Enjoy it. We have another pickup. You might want to stop by the shop and check out the new stuff," she said and headed back to Gus's truck.

"You okay?" Butch asked at the truck door.

"Thinking about Aunt Nellie."

"And your sister and ..." He gave a discreet head tilt toward Gus.

"I'm fine." With a shrug, she lowered her eyes and climbed inside.

Gus took the back roads to Meena's. With the slower speeds, small talk filled the half-hour trip. Loading the etagere didn't take long. Meena had it ready to go, but then she led Mary-Dee to her barn. "I've got some other things set aside for you."

The pair disappeared along with any hope of getting away quickly. Gus looked at Butch and shook his head.

"Game time." Butch waved his phone and went to sit on the screened porch.

Gus moseyed over to the rock wall marking the stairs leading down to the river. He pulled out his phone and called Todd.

Todd answered on the first ring. "Everything okay at Mary-Dee's?"

"We're on a delivery and pick up. A small black vehicle's been following us. I got the plate number. I need you to run it. Virginia plates, Uniform Whiskey Alpha 5582."

"I'm on it." Computer keys clicked in the background. "You find anything suspicious at the shop?"

"Not yet. No time to search for the stationery box. She gave me a key so I can go back over tonight and check more closely. What do you have on Kayley?"

"Nothing. She and Mary-Dee hooked up a couple of years ago. Seems to be a good relationship that frees Mary-Dee, so she doesn't have to close the store when she's needed for suspect sketches somewhere. Why?"

"Just exploring all avenues. What about Aunt Darlene's husband? He been in any more trouble? Or playing cons based on his son's Downs Syndrome?"

His Aunt Darlene's husband, Dwayne, was always into get-rich-quick scams that got him in trouble with the law. With one, Dwayne ended up doing time. They were Gus's family, and he didn't want to believe they'd be messing with international smugglers, but he'd learned never to say never.

"Dwayne's been clean ever since he got out. Butch may have Downs but he's not dumb. He refused to play along with his dad once he got older. I think you're off-base, but it's worth another check."

Mary-Dee and Meena came out the barn door, each with a

box in their arms. Gus shifted his back to them. "Gotta go. Let me know what you find on the plates."

He met them at the truck and lifted the boxes over the wheel tub and onto the bed. "Looks like some good old stuff in these."

Meena's hands flew to her hips. "Watch what you're implying. My stuff is all good and old."

Gus returned a closed-lip smile. Meena considered everything she bought vintage. Even the things from Walmart marked "Made in China" that she bought yesterday.

Meena slipped her arm through Mary-Dee's. "Come see the garden set before you go. Remember how dull and flaky it was? Gus redid it for me. I can't wait for the garden book club members to see it."

"Wow. He did a great job. It looks new. If he ever left the bureau, he could do refinishing."

He slid his hands in his pockets. "Thanks, but I'm not quite ready to quit just yet."

Meena waved the two of them to the seats. "You two sit a spell. I've got lemonade and cookies. Be right back."

"Not very subtle is she." Gus stretched his arms across the back of the garden bench.

"Never was." Mary-Dee settled in the chair across from him. Her gaze met his. "Not gonna happen."

For a flicker of a second, he saw what looked like regret. Just as quickly, she broke eye contact. He changed the subject. "We haven't had a chance to talk about what's going on. Have you felt like someone is watching you?"

"Not really."

"What about customers you don't recognize?"

"We have lots of walk-ins with our location so close to a highway exit. People get off for gas or food, see our sign, and stop in. Happens all the time. So yes, I see lots of strangers."

"Anyone suspicious?"

She shrugged. "A couple of times I've thought something had been shoplifted, but people carry things around thinking they want to buy it then change their mind and put it some place different. I usually find whatever I thought was gone."

"But someone did break in."

"It wasn't a break-in. We accidentally left the door unlocked. It blew open. Nothing was missing. Or moved as far as I could tell. That's why I didn't like that Kayley called Todd."

Stealthily picking up the goods certainly fit the pattern of the smuggling gang.

Or, one of them left the door unlocked on purpose so the smuggler could retrieve the goods.

"Maybe someone from the gang came nosing around for Gianna?"

"I guess it's possible, but except for that first encounter, she's never been to the shop so why would she return? And, I keep saying, not a burglary either. Nothing was missing."

"What about from the till? That old antique cash box would be easy to carry off. It doesn't even lock."

"As you point out, there's no way to lock it, but it's bolted to the counter. I have a small safe in the back for when we make large sales, and I don't leave cash in it overnight. I carry the day's take home until I can get to the bank."

"You keep the cash at your house?" Gus clenched the muscles in his neck in an effort not to lose his temper. "Did any of the bureau security briefings stick with you?"

Her chin hiked up a notch. "I'm always careful."

"Careful about what?" Meena set a large wooden tray with a crystal pitcher on the filigree iron table. Butch carried the matching plate loaded with homemade cookies.

"Gus was lecturing me on security protocol for the shop." Mary-Dee's glare at him grew with every word.

Meena squeezed beside Gus and patted his knee. "Forgive him. He can't help himself. You should listen to his lectures to me." She took the cookie plate from Butch. "Better grab a cookie before he eats 'em all."

"I love your cookies," Butch said around a mouthful of chocolate chip cookie while reaching for another.

Mary-Dee took a glass of lemonade and sipped. "I'm looking forward to book club. Kayley's agreed to watch the shop for me."

"Speaking of the book club, why don't Butch and I move chairs out of the barn while you two ladies chat? I know which ones you use. We can stack them in the screen porch, so they'll be ready to set up later."

"Are you sure you wouldn't rather rest a bit and visit with us?" Meena's bottom lip bowed down like a toddler's caught between anger and anguish.

"I'm good." Gus stood. "Let us know when you're ready to go, Mary-Dee. Come on, Butch."

"Nice escape." Butch slapped his puggy hand on Gus's back when they were out of sight.

Like escape was even possible with the matchmaking Energizer Bunny scampering about. Meena could not get her head wrapped around the fact that he couldn't trust himself to love someone again.

CHAPTER FIVE

GUS HELPED MARY-DEE position the etagere then wandered the shop looking for the stationery box he'd noticed before. He hadn't found it when he came back to the shop that night. Giving up, he went back to the checkout counter.

"Why don't you go on home?" Mary-Dee said to Kayley. "It's almost closing time. No need for all three of us to be here."

"Okay, if, you're sure. There's an auction tonight I want to go to. A new shipment from France. If I get there early, I can look around."

Gus's ears perked up. He'd just received intel about a new shipment of diamonds stolen from a mine in Africa coming in.

Mary-Dee made shooing motions with her hands. "Go, go, and don't forget to keep your eye out for a small desk. I'm still looking."

"I will. Fingers crossed." Kayley raised her hand with crossed fingers.

Mary-Dee tapped her crossed fingers against Kayley's. "See you tomorrow."

"Before you go, did that fancy stationery thing sell?" Gus asked.

Kayley nodded. "Mr. Smyth came in and said it was a perfect gift for his wife's home office. Were you interested in it?"

"Too rich for my pocketbook. Just curious. Good luck at the auction."

The shop bell dinged, and a customer walked in as Kayley walked out. Mary-Dee went off to greet the man.

Gus opened the cash drawer box. A handwritten sales slip showed Mr. Joseph Smyth, with a Kentucky address, paid cash for the stationery box. He snapped a picture with his phone camera and sent it in a text to Todd.

When Mary-Dee joined him behind the sales counter, he showed her the receipt. "Smyth paid cash. Nearly $800 seems like a lot of money to carry around."

"It happens." She busied herself straightening the items on display inside the counter. "What difference does it make?"

"None. I'm surprised, that's all. Is Smyth a regular customer?"

"Kinda. He stops in when he's visiting his son in DC."

Gus slipped the receipt back into the cash box. "Where do you lock up that much cash?"

"I told you I have a small safe in back I use until I take the cash home."

"Is it secure? Maybe that's what they were looking for when they came in the back door."

Her shoulders stiffened. Her hand stilled. "Don't start with me again. Nothing was taken when the back door was left open. I'm not going to let someone waltz in here and rob me. I have protection and can use it as well as you or Todd."

Only he didn't see her using it. She'd bowed out when the Hogan's Alley simulations got too real, opting for sketch work and witness interrogation. She had a keen mind and a gift for re-creating suspects on paper, but no stomach when it came to blood or violence.

"Not arguing, but you are far too trusting. You even have Kayley doing your buying at auction. I'd think you'd want to make your own selections."

She pivoted to face him. Her chin hiked up a notch. "What's with all the questions?"

"Nothing. Just making observations."

She crossed her arms. "Is something going on besides Gianna's disappearance?"

"Not that I know of." He had no choice but to lie, still, the words burned.

"If you say so." Her tone communicated she didn't believe him. "The MS-13 gang doesn't want to harm me. I don't need a bodyguard. They want to silence her. You *guarding* me isn't going to prevent that."

"Maybe, maybe not. But you can't predict what a gang member will do." He'd nearly tipped his hand. He'd have to watch it. "And if we can catch the guys stalking you, maybe we can stop them from harming Gianna."

"*If* there is an MS-13 guy stalking me, I get that. But as far as Kayley goes, she knows what sells as well as I do, and I trust her completely."

For Mary-Dee's sake, he hoped her trust wasn't misplaced.

Twilight faded to dark by the time Mary-Dee locked the shop door for the night. She'd stayed after closing to rearrange furniture in anticipation of Kayley's success at the auction.

Gus refused to leave and stayed to help. Sometimes it was handy to have him around. Other times, like now when he dogged her steps to her car, not so much.

With each step, her irritation grew. At her SUV door, she whirled around and faced him. "I've had enough. This has got to stop."

Gus raised his arms, hands up, palms facing out in a hand

shrug, a smirk on his face.

"Don't give me that look. You know what I mean. You're hovering too close."

"You knew I would be. It's what we talked about with Todd." He pointed to the tote on her arm. "Plus, there's cash in that tote."

She scowled. "I'm not helpless."

He gave a shoulder shrug this time. "Maybe, maybe not. Right now, it's dark and there's protection in numbers."

"DO. NOT. follow me home." She climbed into her SUV and slammed the door.

When she spotted the headlights behind her on the highway moments later, she almost slammed on the brakes to give Gus a scare.

Then she realized the headlights weren't from his truck. Her heartbeat pushed against her ribcage.

Relying on her knowledge of the backroads and her evasion chase training, she managed to lose whoever it was.

She pulled into the garage barn at Aunt Nellie's and quickly closed the automatic door she'd had installed. Her forehead dropped to the steering wheel, and she took a deep breath.

She'd never doubted how dangerous the MS-13 gang was. She'd been on high alert since Gianna went into WITSEC.

But why come after her?

She wasn't the threat. She couldn't offer any information. Gianna hadn't shared anything incriminating with her, and Mary-Dee had no idea where she'd gone.

Her cell rang. Pulling it from the holder on the dashboard, she saw an unidentified number. Her pulse jumped.

"Mary-Dee," she said crisply.

"You protected her once. You won't this time."

Her heart leaped into her throat. The phone slid from her hand, tumbled to the floorboard with a thud. She scrambled to pick it up. The call had disconnected, and there was a crack on the screen, which felt prophetic.

CHAPTER SIX

MARY-DEE'S SUV TAILLIGHTS fed into traffic on the highway and then disappeared. As much as Gus wanted to, he didn't follow her. Todd had assigned a tail who would report any trouble. Gus needed to update Todd on what he'd learned. He pressed Todd's number from his contacts.

Todd answered on the first ring. "Hey."

"You still at the station? We need to talk."

"Heading to The Mill Bar. Meet me there."

"On my way."

The Mill Bar had been their go-to during their college days and Academy training breaks. Todd, Gus, Claudia, and Mary-Dee met up there regularly.

The place looked much the same. It'd been a working grist mill during the settlement of the area. Operation ceased in the seventies, and the abandoned mill became a tourist attraction with a restaurant and tours of the historic grounds. These days, they served non-alcoholic cider and craft beers they brew on-site.

Gus surveyed the interior. The new owners had gussied up

the place. Exposed stone gave a warm, friendly feeling and a long bar of glowing wood invited you to sit a spell. A stone fireplace at one end added ambiance.

Not a large crowd of customers for a Friday night. Four or five sat on bar stools. A table of very happy women shared a platter of wings. At another table, a couple toasted who knew what.

Arriving first, Gus ordered a cider then sat at a table on the patio overlooking the mill wheel and away from listening ears. He made a quick check of the tracker app he'd put on Mary-Dee's vehicle. She was home. He relaxed a bit.

Todd waved when he came in and went directly to the bar for cider, then sat across from Gus. Neither spoke at first.

"To old times." Gus tipped his cider glass.

"I don't think so. Too much has happened since those days." Todd held his glass firmly on the table.

Training forced all recruits at Quantico to reveal dark secrets and deep sorrows to build trust that would make them less vulnerable down the road. From the same hometown, Gus and Todd had a head start.

Then their paths diverged. Todd went back home to local law enforcement. Mary-Dee followed. Gus's failed assignment with Claudia ruined his bond with Mary-Dee and chipped at Todd's confidence in Gus. This forced partnership with her strained their tenuous friendship even more.

"Then to keeping Mary-Dee safe."

Todd raised his glass. "That I can agree to."

Gus clinked his glass to Todd's. He sipped then asked, "Any hits on the plates, or Mary-Dee's customer named Smyth?"

"You were right about him. It is an alias and a rap sheet a mile long starting as a pre-teen. He's cleaned himself up—no more petty, small-time stuff. He's playing with the big boys now and a master of disguise to go with his aliases. You'll receive a copy of the full report we sent to Eric. The plates were from a vehicle stolen two days ago. Still working on that."

"A double bull's eye on her like we thought. MS-13 and Smyth, who is definitely connected to the smuggling gang. Fits the MO. He changes his appearance. We know that." Gus gulped his cider.

"Exactly. The sedan following her, hard to tell, could belong to either."

"My money's on the car being MS-13. No reason for the smugglers to follow her. But with the MS-13 trial starting in a couple of weeks, they've got to stop Gianna from testifying. She does, and those three gang members are going down. Which puts Mary-Dee in a precarious situation without being a smuggling operation suspect for me."

"I agree about the MS-13 threat. But no way is she involved with the smuggling." Todd motioned for the waitress. "I'll have another one of these and the beefsteak burger with everything."

"Same." Gus waited for the waitress to leave. "I agree about Mary-Dee. Eric doesn't know her like we do. He's not willing to discount her as a person of interest yet. You and her still seeing each other?"

"Not anymore. An occasional casual lunch or dinner but nothing serious." There was a hard flash in Todd's eyes as their gazes met. "She'll never be over you."

"Don't be ridiculous. Anything that might have been between us died with Claudia."

"Come on, Gus. Whatever that was with Claudia was an undercover act. Once she knows that, she'll understand."

"I'm not so sure. We had to make it look real. Hardest thing I've had to do was break off with Mary-Dee."

He'd never forget the hurt in her eyes. It haunted his dreams.

"We all believed you. Mary-Dee still does."

"I know. Even if she could forgive my deception, she'll always blame me for Claudia's death."

"Only because you haven't told her the truth. Tell her, same as you told me. And while you're at it, tell your grandmother."

How could he?

He'd always believed he could have done more to protect Claudia. Didn't matter what the official investigation said.

CHAPTER SEVEN

THE MAN'S GAZE followed the woman wandering between the pieces on the crowded auction floor. The bright-colored bandana tied to hold the long coils off her face made her easy to spot.

Hugo laid his bidding paddle on the reserved seat next to hers and went to search for the desk with his next shipment. He'd sat next to her at a couple of auctions before. She flashed a thumbs-up when she saw him.

She was a talker. Filled his ears with tales of her cat, and how her car needed a set of tires, and its transmission was on its last legs. And an online gambling debt, which she did not mention.

A perfect target to be his inside contact.

It had been easy to persuade her to be his agent and bid on pieces for him, which wasn't complicated or suspect. Agents worked for percentages of sale price all the time, especially with online or high-end auctions.

The tricky part had been convincing her and his other patsies to take the objects to the shops where they worked so he could go in and buy them outright. Again, with a promising cut.

That always swayed them.

He counted on her to win the bid on the desk tonight. Once it was at MDR, he'd buy it, unload the diamonds, and take the piece to a different auction to be sold again without any precious cargo inside.

The system he'd come up with had worked at a half dozen shops and auctions from here to Georgia, and north back up the eastern coast to Maryland.

His plan was brilliant.

Convincing the schlemiels had been easy too. The world was full of men and women who needed extra cash and an amazing number of them worked at antique shops.

He'd simply outlined his proposition at that the first auction when he met them. "Before we start, you've heard of agents who buy for others, right? Would you be interested in being my agent?"

Not one failed to agree after Hugo explained what their percentage would be. "For real," they'd say with wide eyes. He'd wink and flash a sly grin and reel in his unsuspecting mule.

Just like he had this one.

"Everyone be seated, please. We have a lot of good stuff to move tonight. Bidding starts in ten minutes," the auctioneer announced on the PA bringing Hugo's reminiscence to an end.

People scuttled for their seats. The woman sat beside him.

"Glad to see you again, Hugo." She extended her hand.

He took it, placing his other hand atop hers. "Good to be here. Let's hope the pickings are good tonight."

"How're your farmhouse renovations coming?"

"Remodeling is always slow."

"You're planning to flip it?"

"Nah. It's more a hobby." *And a cover.*

The auctioneer's voice came from the podium high above the chattering bidders. "Our first item tonight is this lovely Welsch hutch."

Two of his helpers carried the dark wood hutch with its narrow plate rack top to the center of the room, frontside forward then flipped it so the back was visible. They paused in center front to give the bidders a good view.

"Do I hear $300?" Paddles rose. The auctioneer shouted the amounts as the numbers rose.

Hugo shook his head when she asked if he wanted her to bid. "Too much."

Nor was it the piece with his cargo.

Hours later, she had bid on nothing, neither had he. The one piece he wanted hadn't come up.

The woman stood. "I'm giving up. This is wasting my time."

"Not a good night, 'ay?" He struggled to keep his own frustration out of his voice.

"Nope. Things are going way too high for us to re-sell at the shop. Same thing happened last Friday. I'm going home. What about you?"

"Nothing really strikes my fancy either."

She stood. "I'll try again next week. See you then." She followed other bidders to the exit.

Hugo squeezed the canned drink in his hand until it crackled and collapsed. His foreign boss would not be happy. He clutched the wad of cash in his pocket and headed to the staging area.

He'd slip some cash to the auction helpers to move the piece he wanted out of the lineup for tonight's auction. Save it for next week. Shouldn't be a big problem, these workers also needed a bit of extra cash.

Only the piece he planned to bid on wasn't among the lineup of furniture to be auctioned tonight. This was not good.

He pulled his phone from his pocket and called his dock contact. "Where's the desk? It's not here."

The voice replied, "A container got held up in customs."

What the hell? "What do you mean held up in customs?"

"Something on the manifest triggered a look through the entire container. We gotta wait for them to unpack and inspect everything on the manifest then re-pack before it moves off the dock."

"How long's that gonna take?"

"One-two days, a week. Who knows? Only two customs workers are unloading. They said they had to look at every-thing. Lots of stuff. I'm watching and it's not a speedy process. I let Europe know. We can't do anything without drawing attention."

"Call me the minute the container leaves the dock," Hugo growled and disconnected.

He had no choice. He'd come back when the desk was moved to the auction house and nudge the woman toward bidding again. That wouldn't be hard.

Convincing his diamond buyer to wait might take more persuasion.

Unless customs found the diamonds. That would be a whole different ballgame.

The guys in Europe better have hidden them well.

CHAPTER EIGHT

MARY-DEE GREETED KAYLEY the next morning at the shop. There was no smile on her face. The auction must have been a bust. "No luck?"

"Worse night ever. Sorry I'm late. I overslept," Kayley said on her way to put her lunch in the fridge in the back. When she returned, she added, "Everything went so high we couldn't make any money. I kept hoping and stayed way later than I should have."

"It's always luck with auctions. Sometimes great stuff, low bids. Other times awful. It's why I gave up on auctions. My best picking is at estate sales. I'm sorry you wasted your time. I'm thankful you're willing to go."

"I love 'em. It feeds my gambling urge without costing me. Sometimes we make good money on something I win. Just not last night. You heading to the estate sales now?"

Mary-Dee lifted her purse from beneath the counter. "Front Royal first, then Winchester. Fingers crossed I find good stuff."

"Find what?" Gus breezed through the shop door.

"Stuff at the estate sales. Last night's auction was a total bust. We're hoping she'll have better luck," Kayley answered.

His eyes zeroed on Mary-Dee's. "Am I riding with you or following?"

She heaved a sigh. She was already tired of having Gus around. It seemed like months, not days. On the other hand, after last night's call, having him around might be a good thing.

"I'll drive since you need GPS backup and don't have AC in your truck." She waved at Kayley and headed to the door.

Gus trailed behind her.

"What'd Kayley mean the auction was a bust?" Gus settled into the passenger seat and rested his elbow on the soft leather console.

"Bids went high, and they announced one of the containers never arrived."

One of the containers didn't make it. Was that planned? Not that he was aware. He'd have to check with Eric when Mary-Dee wasn't around.

She strapped her seat belt in place and held her back stiff as she positioned her hands at ten and two like a poster for driver training. "She normally has good luck so last night was a total bust." She merged into traffic.

"Meena always said auctions were unpredictable. On the other hand, the snack bars have great hot dogs. I love those dogs. You did too, remember? Might be worth going to an auction to try another one."

"Not me. I have better luck at estate sales." Her subtext being not with him.

Her eyes shifted to the rearview mirror for the third time since they'd gotten on the highway. Her knuckles were white on the steering wheel, had been since they'd started.

Something was bothering her. He checked the side mirror. Watched for a few minutes. No tail.

"Everything okay? You seem a little tense."

"I'm fine." She turned to flash a frown at him. "I'd be better if this stupid trial were over, and you weren't dogging my every step."

"We all will."

"Gianna isn't going to contact me. You and whoever is watching me are wasting your time."

"What do you mean *whoever is watching you*?"

"Nothing."

Mary-Dee exited the highway and navigated a left-hand turn at the sign marking the estate sale. He peered at his side mirror. A dark sedan followed. Different plate numbers than before.

Another antiquer or tail? He couldn't be sure.

She parked off the grass and checked her mirrors again. She'd been checking the mirrors as much as he had. He rested his hand on her forearm. "What makes you think someone is following you?"

"I don't." She flipped his hand away and slid out her door.

He waited until she rounded the car, walked beside her, and before she had her lucky hat settled on her head, asked, "You were never good at lying. What's happened?"

"Nothing." A long silent beat held until her shoulders slumped. "I got a call last night."

Gus stepped in front of her. "Why didn't you call me or Todd?"

She raised her hand in a stop signal. "The call lasted all of fifteen seconds. No point. We both know tracking is next to impossible on short calls. No way at all to triangulate. Besides, I'm sure he used a burner and pitched it as soon as he hung up."

"It was a *he*?"

"I'm using the generic he. Whoever it was used a voice-altering device. I couldn't tell."

"Let me see your phone." He extended his hand.

"This is ridiculous," she muttered.

"Your phone. Now."

Her lips narrowed to a thin line as she dug into her purse. "Here." She thrust the phone at him.

Not an iPhone. An old dumb phone, a step above a burner. She probably never ran updates either. Her aversion to technology hadn't changed. He understood. Her sketches were often better than the computer's images.

He turned the old phone on, waited for it to load up. "The screen's cracked. How'd that happen?"

"Hearing that voice ..." She swallowed. "It scared me ... I dropped it."

"I'm calling Todd."

"Fine. I'm going to do what I came here to do." She whirled around and headed for the line of shoppers waiting to go inside.

Gus texted the phone conversation to Todd then called him. "The MS-13 goons don't know Mary-Dee. She doesn't threaten easily. Their call only made her more determined to help if Gianna does contact her."

"You're right. We'll need her phone so I can get IT on this, but it's a long shot at best."

"We're at an estate sale now. We'll bring it in later. Check on what I sent until then."

"After this, I think we can say for sure the car following her is MS-13. Not your smuggler."

"But he is around with his goons. I can feel it."

And so were those MS-13 thugs. He scanned the parked cars, slid his phone back into his pocket, and hustled to find Mary-Dee.

Gus caught up with her in the line waiting to go inside and handed her phone back. "Todd wants your phone. We can drop it off on our way to the next sale. For now, relax. We used to have a fun time antiquing with Aunt Nellie and Meena."

"That was a long time ago."

"True, but not impossible again. What are we looking for today?"

"I'm not sure. Whatever strikes my fancy. I was expecting Kayley to bring in a couple of pieces of furniture. I need stuff to fill the holes at the shop."

Once upon a time, Gus had wanted to be her *fancy*. No more. After what happened, he couldn't trust himself to love anyone. He swallowed the longing growing in his chest for what might have been. He was here to protect her or prove she'd become a smuggler. No room for fancies.

"Are you shopping for yourself or picking?" The woman behind them asked, and Mary-Dee turned away.

"I have a shop," Mary-Dee answered.

"Where's your shop?" The woman's question drew Mary-Dee's attention away from Gus. She focused on her conversation with the lady behind her in line until the official at the door waved them inside.

"Good luck. I'll stop in your shop some time."

Gus took her hand. The familiarity pinged her heart. She slipped her fingers from his. He was only here for his job. Not her. And if she kept saying it enough, she might believe it.

She had too much on her mind to think about the good times with Gus or her growing attraction to the man she'd once loved. She definitely didn't want to admit between the tail and last night's call she was glad he was with her.

He pulled her toward the downstairs bathroom with a broad grin. "We always had fun in powder rooms and found good stuff."

"I'm not interested in fun stuff. Resell stuff is this way." She tugged him toward the kitchen.

A few minutes later, he reached into a high kitchen cabinet and pulled down a complete set of blue depression glass mixing bowls.

"How's this?" His enlarged dark irises sparkled with delight and an awareness she recognized. He was feeling whatever was growing between them too.

"A slam dunk. Thank you very much. I'd never have spotted it way up there."

She took the much sought-after set from his hands already thinking of several customers who would want to snatch up the rare find. She ran her fingers around the edges to check for chips and cracks then handed it back to him. "Will you start a shelf for us at checkout?"

"Yes, ma'am," he said. A familiar warm feeling seeped through her body when he covered her hands as he took the bowls from her. There was a faint smile on his face. "Be right back."

Gus caught up with her in the formal dining room where glassware and figurines lined tables, two china cabinets, and the top of a gorgeous Black Forest hunt cabinet. "Will you look at that? You've always wanted a hunt cabinet. I wonder if it's for sale?"

One of the estate sales employees watching the crowds stood next to the cabinet. "It is and we'll even throw in free delivery."

Mary-Dee ran her hand over the carved drawer pulls. "It's gorgeous and in great shape. A little too pricey for me or my shop."

She moved to the smaller curved glass cabinet across the room and looked inside.

Slowly, they made their way through each room of the house. When their arms were loaded, Gus carried her finds to their shelf at checkout and returned.

"This is the last area." Mary-Dee opened the back door. Yard art wasn't her thing, but a good garden set like Meena found at Darlene's would sell in a heartbeat. Two steps outside, she scanned the space, twirled around, and bumped into his chest.

He steadied her. A tinge of electricity shot up her arm and she stepped around him, head down. "There's nothing out here that fits for the shop. We can leave."

"Good thing. You're out of space on your buyer's shelf." She heard the smile in his voice.

"I do want to have one more look at the hunt cabinet, though."

His smile became a choked laugh. "I figured you would."

She spotted the sold sign and shook her head sadly. "Too late. Someone bought it already." Disappointment laced her words.

"Me. For you." Gus lifted the sold card and flipped it over to show his name written on the back. "You need to give them delivery instructions."

"You bought it?"

"What'd Meena teach us? 'The time to buy an antique is when you see it.' You've always wanted one. We both know hunt cabinets are hard to find and this one is outstanding."

Mary-Dee blinked and blinked. She couldn't believe he'd done that. She grabbed his sleeve and tugged him off to the side away from the seller's ears.

"Why would you do that?"

"I owe you more than a hunt cabinet, but it's a start." She didn't want to hear the regret in his voice or the unspoken appeal for forgiveness.

"It's too expensive."

"I can afford it. Undercover work doesn't provide much opportunity to spend my money."

Her chin dipped and her shoulders sank. "Still, I can't accept it."

A look of disappointment transformed the glow on his face

to hurt. "Okay," he said, his voice soft, laced with remorse. "I understand."

She hoped he did. No way was she ready to accept gifts from him. She went to the checkout area to pay for her purchases.

Since he'd reappeared in her life, she'd seen a different Gus Nolan. What happened with Claudia had affected him as much as her. He was more grounded, less impulsive. Stubborn and mule-headed as ever, but certainly more reasonable than before.

But was it genuine or a performance for his job of protecting her?

CHAPTER NINE

THE ESTATE SALESPERSON removed the SOLD sign from the Black Forest hunt cabinet. "She doesn't want it. I guess that means it's not sold."

Gus handed him his card. "I said I'd buy it, and I will. Call when you're ready to deliver. We can set up a time."

Meena says there's always room for one more thing in the barn. Guess he'd find out if she was right.

He didn't understand Mary-Dee's refusal. She'd talked about wanting a hunt cabinet forever. Even pointed out pictures of them in Meena's price reference guides. She'd described the exact one she wanted down to the last detail of fox head drawer pulls all those years ago. "Someday I'll see one and I'll buy it," she'd said often enough.

Today, her eyes glowed when she spotted the cabinet. Her voice had gone all wistful. This one met all her criteria except it had bear head pulls, not foxes. So, why had she balked? It wasn't about bears instead of foxes.

The morning had been fun, and easy. No talk of the missing girl or the past. They'd laughed, joked, enjoyed themselves like old times. He'd thought the boundaries were coming down.

A part of him knew he was kidding himself. He'd goofed. Misread her signals. It was too soon. His need for Mary-Dee's forgiveness had made him misinterpret her smiles, her touches, her laughter. Bottom line, she still didn't trust him. Until she did, she would never forgive him.

He had to remember that and stick to his job, abandon anything else.

Gus gave the cashier his credit card at the checkout station, gathered Mary-Dee's bags, and shadowed her out to her car.

"I apologize." He lifted her bags into the opened hatch. "I overstepped. It won't happen again."

"Thank you." She pressed the button on her key fob to lower the rear of her SUV.

His eyes scanned the parked cars. Two rows over he spotted two large, tattooed men getting into a dark sedan. He put his hand up to stop the hatch door's descent.

"Over there." Giving a head tilt in the direction of the black sedan, he leaned closer to her. "They've picked up your tail again. Act like you're checking your purchases. I'm going to sneak around and get a picture of the occupants."

She didn't argue. "Go."

Crouching low, he angled toward the black sedan and snapped photos with his phone when he got close enough. Mary-Dee was talking to another shopper when he returned to her car.

"Gus, this is Hazel, another dealer friend of mine. We seem to end up at the same estate sales often." Her eyes voiced the unspoken question, "Did you get a picture?"

He gave a twitch of a nod. "Nice to meet you, Hazel. Any luck today?"

"Not as much as Mary-Dee. Maybe I'll catch you two at the

next one." The woman, who looked to be Meena's age, trotted away like a bouncy teenager clutching her purchases.

"You ready to go now?" Mary-Dee asked.

Gus nodded. "I texted the photos to Todd. We still need to get your phone to IT at the station. We'll drop it off on the way to the next sale."

"I told you—"

"And I'm telling you, techs these days can do things they couldn't dream of when you were an agent. They need your phone. Plus, Todd may have an ID on our tail by the time we get there."

The drive to the Mount Pleasant Police Station was like riding in a hearse, quiet and slow. Cars filled with people leaving DC for a weekend in the Virginia countryside made for busy traffic. That she'd given in accounted for the lack of conversation on Mary-Dee's part.

She was not happy. This useless trip meant she'd miss the second estate sale. The techs were not going to find anything on her phone that would give a clue as to who made the threatening call.

At least, Gus had the good sense not to try and start a conversation.

The IT guy met them at Todd's office. He took one look at Mary-Dee's phone. "I'm not sure we'll get anything off this. It's so old."

"Give it your best shot," Todd said.

"See, I told you," Mary-Dee hissed at Gus.

"If you had a smartphone, they'd have better luck. But they may find something."

"I don't need a smartphone. Mine works just fine. Thank you very much. I don't chase the newest techie thing like you do."

"At least it's not a flip phone or your old Blackberry," Gus countered.

Todd cleared his throat loudly. "Children, that's enough. We have a hit on the photo Gus sent." Another officer handed him a sheet of paper.

He passed the mugshot to Mary-Dee. "Recognize him?"

She didn't. He looked like every other suspect she'd sketched. Mean and dangerous. All those MS-13 tattoos made him look even scarier.

"Never seen him before."

Todd took the sheet from her. "Okay then. We'll put out an APB and circulate copies to our patrol cars."

Mary-Dee's frustration level came to a boil. "You think that's going to stop them? They'll just send someone else."

"You're right. It won't stop them," Gus answered. "But it could slow them up if we get to them and one of them talks. Any delay might help her get away."

"I'm surprised Gianna's managed to evade them this long. I'm so afraid they're going to find her."

"Me too." Todd nodded in agreement.

Mary-Dee looked at her watch and ground her back teeth. She'd never make the second estate sale. "If that's all you need from me, I'm going back to the shop."

"Wait." Gus stopped her. "Not without a phone. Techs are keeping yours. Todd, you have any burners around?"

"Just so happens we have a bunch down in the evidence room. Some guy had a duffle full when we arrested him. All new, unused. I'll grab one for her."

"Great. Then we can head out." Gus gave her one of his smug nods.

She crossed her arms firmly to her chest. "No. I've had enough for one day. Todd will find you another way back for your truck."

The room went silent. Gus stood stunned but didn't argue.

Todd returned and handed her the burner. "You're all set."

"Thanks." She gave a stage smile. "I'm off. Alone. Gus will need a ride."

Todd's eyes went from her to Gus and back to her. The bump of his Adam's apple rode up then down his slender neck. "Okay. Sure."

The door of his office banged closed, and she wove her way through the squad room to the exit.

Gus rubbed his fingers up and down the center of his forehead. "Put a squad car on her, please."

"Got it." Todd signaled the desk sergeant and pointed toward Mary-Dee's rapidly disappearing body. The sergeant nodded.

"What'd you do to set her off this time?"

"Tried to buy her a hunt cabinet." Gus slid into the chair in front of Todd's desk.

"A hunt cabinet?"

"You remember that hutchy thing from the Black Forest that has all the animal carvings? The one she always talked about wanting. There was one at the estate sale this morning. I bought it for her."

Todd's eyebrows rose. "You bought it for her? Bet that went over well."

Gus gave a boisterous laugh that had heads lifting in the squad room. "Ya think? Can I get a patrol car to drop me off for my truck?"

"Sam will take you." Todd called, and the young recruit came over. "Don't go telling him about how much better it is to go with the Bureau than a local station."

"Right." Gus winked and draped his arm over the young officer's shoulders.

Todd gave Gus's shoulder a brotherly squeeze. "And give Mary-Dee a break. All this is messing with her too. Go home. Our patrol has it covered."

CHAPTER TEN

SATURDAYS AT MDR Antiques could be a boom or a bust. Today was one of those slow Saturdays. Not even any "tire-kickers" as she called the ones who only came to browse, drink her coffee, and eat her cookies.

Mary-Dee had made one sale after she'd returned to the shop, a 1910 postcard for a whopping eight dollars. Kayley had almost talked a repeat customer into the marble top dresser she came to look at for the fourth time. Maybe next time the woman would finally walk out with the 1850s walnut piece.

She looked at the clock again. Three forty-five. Another hour and fifteen minutes till closing. Entirely too much time. Kayley had been pelting her with questions about Gus.

"Gus hasn't come in. You two have a new fight?"

Mary-Dee laughed. "No. Not a new fight. The same one. He's hovering and I think it's unnecessary. Todd has a patrol car stationed outside."

Trying to escape any more questions, she walked over to the mini coffee bar.

The coffee machine offered a variety of blends and there

were homemade cookies beneath a glass dome pedestal dish. Customers welcomed the treats and lingered. The longer they did, the more likely they were to buy something, according to a marketing article she'd read.

Sometimes the strategy worked, sometimes it didn't. They'd eat the cookies and drink the coffee and leave without making a purchase.

Kayley followed her and lifted the cookie cover. "I get the idea there's more to this than his bodyguard gig. Weren't you and Gus an item in the past?"

"Ancient past, and that's where it stays." Mary-Dee dropped the tiny pod into the coffee maker and pressed the lever.

"I'm not so sure about that." Kayley rolled her eyes. "I see the way he looks at you. It's more than a job for him. You look at him the same way sometimes when he's not looking. Me thinks things could be changing."

"Never. Not going to happen."

Unfortunately, his presence did make her heart doubt her words. Every time she felt herself slipping, she mentally reviewed the moment the agents came to tell her Claudia was dead. That usually vanquished any warm fuzzies for Gus Nolan.

She added a lid to the paper cup. "Listen, would you mind if I cut out and left closing to you? It's been a long, frustrating day."

"Frustrating? I'd say frightening. Two gang members tailing you."

"They're not after me. They're looking for Gianna, and they're crazy to think she'll come to me. Or I would lead them to her."

"Still, you've had a scary time of it today. Go home and take a long hot soak in that gorgeous footed tub of yours. I'll close here then head over to the auction house to see if the container has been released for tomorrow night's auction."

"Thanks. You're a godsend." Mary-Dee hugged Kayley then gathered her purse and carried her coffee to her SUV.

Forty minutes later, she crossed the covered bridge fully

intending to head down the road to her house and doing what Kayley suggested. But the river looked so calm and inviting that she pulled off the road to watch the sunset and wrestle with a boatload of conflicting emotions. Once she got those back under control, she'd go home and take that soak.

She locked her things in the SUV, slid her keys into her pocket, and wandered down the slope. A long time ago, she and Gus had rolled a log to the water's edge. Sitting on it, she pulled off her shoes and flipped her legs over to wiggle her toes in the refreshing water.

The MS-13 trial was scheduled to start on Monday. Not a minute too soon. She so wanted all this to be over. Gianna safe. Gus gone.

A twig snapped behind her. Dread did a spider crawl up her spine. Was it Gus jogging by again? She did not want to see him anymore today.

She whipped around and faced the man in the mugshot. All those tat marks were a dead giveaway. The MS-13 gang name tattoo on his arm and the classic three dots on his hand. The devil's head with a halo and two horns peeking at her from his partially buttoned black shirt confirmed his identity.

"Where is she?" he asked.

No visible gun, but she knew he had one. And a knife. These MS-13 guys always carried both, she remembered from agency intel.

"I have no idea," she answered in an admirably steady, normal voice considering she'd locked her knees to keep from crumbling.

"I don't believe you." His husky Hispanic voice carried a heavy accent, but his English syntax was excellent. He wasn't a street thug. More likely a higher-up in the food chain specifically hired for his skill at discouraging witnesses.

"I can't help that. I haven't seen Gianna since she ran into my shop then disappeared."

"Liar! You were the sketch artist who helped get Alejandro and the others arrested."

"True, we did meet at the police station. It was hardly a personal visit."

Stepping forward, his hand slid behind his back and came forward with a .380 pointed at her.

At the same time, she caught a movement by the big oak tree. Gus ran at the guy from behind and toppled him to the ground. The gun flew in the air and landed several feet from the fighting pair.

Mary-Dee raced over, picked the weapon up, and fired it in the air. "Stop."

The gang member used the distraction to wrap his arm around Gus's neck and point a knife blade at his aortic vein.

"Drop it or I kill him."

"Or I can shoot you." She prayed he didn't hear the quiver in her words. "I'm a former FBI agent."

"Right. I'm scared." His lips curled in a smirk.

He began to back away, slowly dragging Gus with him.

Mary-Dee aimed and squeezed the trigger. The bullet struck his shoulder. His knife tumbled to the ground.

At the same time, Gus jabbed his elbow into the guy's gut and twisted from his grip. Twirling around, Gus kneed him in the groin. The gang member tumbled to the ground like a rockslide.

Gus jerked the guy's hands behind his back and secured them with his belt.

Her gaze went up the bank. "Does he have a partner?"

"Secured. He won't be waking up for a while. Call Todd."

Within seconds, sirens wailed in the distance, and a patrol car skidded to a stop behind her SUV. Sam and his older partner raced down the embankment. "We weren't far away on the other side of the covered bridge."

Gus motioned toward the gang member on the ground. "Gunshot to the shoulder. He'll need an ambulance."

Sam pressed the button on his shoulder radio. "Cancel backup. Suspect down and wounded. Send an ambulance."

He gave Gus an admiring grin. "You took him down?"

"Not me." Gus pointed to Mary-Dee. "She did. I got the one in the car. He never saw what hit him."

He came toward her. "You are still one sharpshooting Annie Oakley. You okay?"

"Fine." Her knees wobbled and buckled under her.

Gus caught her before she hit the ground.

Seconds later, she opened her eyes to Gus's face. Their gazes clung for a long moment, and she felt as if whatever had kept them apart suddenly fractured. Thoughts she didn't need, didn't want, filled her head. She squeezed her eyes closed again.

No! That part of her life was over. Done.

The ambulance arrived. The doors flew open, and the EMTs came rushing down.

"I got this one." Gus dipped his chin to Mary-Dee in his arms then did a head tilt toward Sam with the wounded guy. "Gunshot. And there's another one in the car. Concussion."

"I can walk." Mary-Dee shoved from his arms. She swayed as soon as her feet hit the ground.

Gus scooped her up again. "I'm not so sure about that. Let's get you checked out."

Todd met them at the ambulance. "Good job, Gus."

"Not me. Mary-Dee. She saved my neck … literally."

She slid from his arms, lifted her shoulders, cobbling a professional mask. "Told you I could take care of myself."

Gus wasn't convinced. She'd held tight enough that he could feel her shaking as he carried her up the embankment. Inhaling the scent of her skin, he'd never wanted to turn her loose.

Todd gave her a tight squeeze. "This could have gone so differently. I'm happy you two still work so well as a team. I'll need your statements as soon as the EMT clears you."

With a nod, she followed the EMT.

"At least this time we won't have to do all the paperwork," Gus said to her retreating back.

"She okay?" Todd asked.

"As okay as you get when you've just shot someone. He thought he'd scare her into telling him where Gianna was. She outfoxed him."

The EMTs carried the gang member past. He shot the finger at Gus.

Gus's nostrils flared. The vein in his temple pounded like a kettle drum. Fire reignited in his belly as he took a step forward.

Todd's arm slapped across his chest. "Calm down."

Calm down? She could have died.

One of the EMTs tapped his arm. "Sir, I need to look at your neck now. Come with me."

Once inside the ambulance, the EMT tipped Gus's head for a closer look at his neck. "Fortunately, it's only a scratch. This may sting."

Gus flinched as the disinfectant smoothed the wound and cooled his anger to a low flame.

With his neck bandaged and instructions to follow up with his physician, Gus joined Mary-Dee and Todd at her SUV.

"You'll both need to come down to the station to give your statements. Now, or in the morning."

Gus gave a shrug.

"Now works for me." Mary-Dee nodded a thanks to Sam and leaned against the fender to slide into the shoes he'd brought her.

"Fine with me then. Can I catch a ride with you?" Gus asked.

"She rides with me. You bring her SUV," Todd answered.

"Whatever." Gus held out his hand for her keys.

She dug in her pocket and came up empty. "I must have dropped them."

"You two go on. I'll find 'em and meet you there."

Todd's arm circled her shoulders, and he led her to his squad car. A quick, nasty twinge Gus pegged as jealousy torqued inside his chest. He grabbed the nearest officer's flashlight and headed down the embankment.

CHAPTER ELEVEN

GIVING HIS STATEMENT didn't take much time. Gus waited in Todd's office while Mary-Dee finished hers. She flashed a wry smile as she walked in.

"Looks like I'll have to take you home. Todd says he can't spare a patrol car tonight. Something about a full moon bringing out the crazies."

"I could call Meena if it's a problem." He'd rather ride with her, but he *could call his grandmother.*

"It's late. No need to wake her. She'll want a full explanation for why you're here which means a rehash of what happened. I'm not ready for that. I'm sure you're not either. I'll drop you off and head home for a long overdue soak in my tub."

"Sounds like an excellent plan." He kept his voice steady, smooth while he struggled to squelch the vision in his head of her in a claw-footed tub covered with bubbles. He was having enough trouble managing the lingering feel of her in his arms for the first time in years.

Waving her keys, he added, "You'll need these."

"Thank you." A ghost of a smile touched her lips. He chose

to believe it was for more than finding her car keys.

Their walk to her car was quiet. Twight light had given way to dusk. A full moon rose shedding moonlight where there were no streetlights. Under different circumstances, he'd guide her to the gazebo in the park between the police station and city hall then sit to talk like they'd done when they were teenagers. Unfortunately, his lies – past and present – ruined that option.

"Thank you for saving my life tonight." He broke the silence once they were on the highway to his home.

"I could say the same. He would have shot me because I wouldn't have given him the information he wanted even if I had it."

"We worked as a team and that's what gave this situation a positive ending."

Conversation died again until Mary-Dee guided the vehicle slowly across the covered bridge. The tires thrummed across the wooden planks like a music box winding down.

On the other side of the bridge, she stopped and rested her chin on the steering wheel to stare down at the place that held so many good memories for them both.

"It'll never be the same." There was a tremor in her voice.

They'd shared their first kiss under that giant oak tree, spent hours talking, planning a future together.

He reached across to squeeze her hand. "We can't let that happen. We'll build new memories."

Even as he said it, he knew until he told her the truth about what happened in Florida, why he'd stayed away, and the real reason why he'd come back, there'd always be a chasm between them. A lack of trust.

"I'm afraid it's too late." Her voice filled with such sorrow his heart hurt.

This could be his chance to at least come clean about Claudia. For the last minutes of the ride to his house, he stewed in teenage angst about how to tell her the true story of Florida.

His hand hesitated on the door handle when she pulled to a stop at his barndominium door. "Why don't you come in? We can decompress together over a cup of coffee like we used to do in our bureau days."

Her hands slid around and around the edge of the steering wheel as she considered her answer.

"Come on. It'd help us both," he prompted.

Her eyes closed. She turned off the ignition. "Might as well, I'm not going to sleep anyway."

He wasn't sure if the vibes he felt coming from her were only from what they'd been through or apprehension about being back in the place where they'd spent so much time together.

Key in hand, he slid from her car. Hope lightened his steps, only to be tempered by the knowledge that the truth would be difficult for her to hear. He had no idea how'd she react.

Mary-Dee leaned down to pet the dog waiting at his front door. "You got a dog?"

"No. She wandered up during a rainstorm. Soaked and looked hungry despite being so fat. I let her in and fed her." He gave an exasperated sigh. "Now she won't go away."

Mary-Dee rubbed her hand along the dog's side. "She's not fat, Gus. I think she's pregnant."

"She's fat. All the neighbors have been feeding her too," he said as the dog darted its way between them and headed straight for the dog bed in front of the fireplace.

"I can't believe you allow her inside. You always said you'd never have a sissy housedog."

"She's not staying forever. I couldn't leave her outside. Not with all the rain we've had."

He went to the kitchen area and put on coffee. While it brewed, he set mugs on the concrete countertop of the bar separating the living area from the kitchen lined with steel grey cabinets. "Still like cream and sugar?"

Mary-Dee nodded. "So, what do you call your she's-not-staying-dog?"

She pointed to the dog dishes at the end of the counter.

He hadn't considered a name for her. Naming something meant an official connection. Anything he'd loved had left him. His parents. Claudia. Mary-Dee. No point in becoming attached to Dog. If he gave her a name, she'd disappear as fast as she'd appear.

He didn't say any of that. He answered, "I don't call her anything. I'm trying to find a home for her with very little luck, but she's not staying here."

Her eyes fixed on his. "Hm-mm. Then you need to take her to the vet and be sure she's not pregnant. If she is, you'll be fighting a losing battle. I have a friend who's in rescue. Finding a foster for a pregnant dog is nearly impossible. County shelters might take her if you want to leave her at a kill shelter."

"No. I'll find a home for her." He turned back to the coffee maker and filled two mugs.

She reached for the mug he offered. The coffee sloshed a bit. She circled the cup with her other hand and pulled back.

"Aftershocks. Your adrenaline is sliding back to normal. To be expected."

"I remember." She moved to the couch.

Dog came to lay on her feet. Its muzzle rested at her ankles. She motioned to his mug. "Your hand's steady. No after-shocks?"

"I've learned to deal with them." Gus sat in the large leather recliner across from her, sipped his coffee.

"I never could. It's one of the reasons I left. Besides ..." Her gaze fell to her coffee mug.

"I understand. It's time you know the truth about Claudia and me. Why I've stayed away."

All he could think when he'd seen that gun pointed at Mary-Dee was she'd die believing a lie. Timing wasn't ideal but this might be his only opportunity to unload the secret he'd been keeping and pray she'd forgive him.

Mary-Dee threw up her chin, yanked her feet from under the dog, and stood. "I don't want to talk about that."

He crossed to her, placed his hand around her arm. She jerked against his hold. He relaxed his fingers but didn't let go. "Please stay. You don't know the whole story about Florida."

"I do. Todd told me."

"No. Todd told you what I wanted you to hear, then. You need to know the truth now." He owed her that much even if his undercover reason for being here would have to wait.

With a fulminating glare, she angled to face him and hissed through clamped teeth. "That wasn't the truth?"

"No. It was better to have you blame me. Until today, I hadn't thought it mattered. You could have died this afternoon, and I realized I don't want to lose you believing a lie. You need to know what went down."

For several long seconds, she glowered at him before she crossed her arms and sat back down stiffly. Her expression morphed somewhere between suspicion and confusion. "So, tell me."

"Today, when you shot that gang member, you acted on the information you had and saved us both. In Florida, I made a choice that turned out to be wrong and I lost everything. Claudia. You."

"What do you mean?" Unreadable eyes shifted to his.

"For the undercover job, we were set up as a married couple to infiltrate a smuggling operation based in Florida. What I let you believe was that I betrayed you for your sister. But the truth is I never stopped loving you."

Her hand flexed and released. "You did a convincing job."

"It was necessary. The gang's tentacles ran deep. I didn't want you at risk. I never loved Claudia, not like that, but I could never tell you."

"She always loved you as much as I did. It was easy to believe she'd lured you away. Why did you let me continue to believe it was real after she died?"

"To protect you. Because scenarios like tonight happen far too often. Whether you know anything or not if the bad guy believes you do, that can lead to disaster."

"I'll give you that." Her chin dipped. Her eyes drifted down and to the right. She was remembering their good times. Her lips tightened then she raised her chin. "How did Claudia die if it didn't go down like Todd told me?"

Gus raised his coffee mug. Empty. Needing fuel but unwilling to go to the kitchen to refill it, he swallowed hard and continued, "Claudia absorbed herself in our roles. She loved the setup — lives of the rich and famous. All the wine and fine dining, the trips on yachts, the flights to exotic places just for dinner. You know your sister. She flirted and teased ... and fell in love with the son of the smuggling leader."

He gave her a couple of seconds for that to soak in. "She didn't hide it from me. Quite the opposite, she demanded to be released from the operation so they could be together. I told her she was crazy. She'd get herself killed. She refused to listen."

Mary-Dee's cheeks went from pale to practically gray. She gasped.

"She wasn't to be stopped. I was sure it would be a disaster. I couldn't convince Claudia, or the son, that his father would never allow the heir-apparent to leave. She refused to concede and went to our handler with her plan for the son to become an informant in exchange for immunity. We were anxious to bring this guy down and they bought her plan. My protests fell on deaf ears."

Gus set his mug down and leaned forward, propping his elbows on his knees, and clasped his hands together prayerlike, rubbing his chin back and forth over his knuckles before he took a deep breath. "The day they planned to meet on the son's yacht to go away together, I followed her. She handed her suitcase over to the steward, climbed on board, and into the heir apparent's arms. I jumped on board as the yacht pulled away. That's when bullets started flying."

Guilt and grief washed through him. He scrubbed his hands down his cheek, closed his eyes, and opened them slowly before he went on. "The son went down. So did Claudia. I rushed to her. The next shot took me down. I lay with my ear on her chest. I heard her stop breathing and thought that would be the last thing I would ever hear. The shooter kicked my side and flipped me over, straddling me with his gun barrel at my forehead. I woke up in the hospital a week later. Claudia was dead. The son was dead. My cover blown."

He rested his head on the back of the couch, his voice carried a tremor. "I should have died that day too rather than spending months at Walter Reed recovering. Nothing will bring your sister back and it's my fault."

Silence spread through the room like the dust from an IED explosion. His heartbeat roared in his chest. Dog moved across to him and dropped her snout onto his knee. Gus rubbed her head, afraid to look at Mary-Dee.

He heard her rise. No shouting. No sob. Nothing. Her quietness bore down like a tombstone.

The front door clicked open and closed again. Tears gathered in his eyes. He swallowed them down. Once he was sure she was far enough down the road that she wouldn't see him, he grabbed his truck keys.

Dog trotted up to the door with him. "No. You stay." He rubbed her head. "It's going to be a long night."

CHAPTER TWELVE

BONG. BONG. BONG.

Mary-Dee heard the Grandmother clock in the hall strike three a.m. She'd counted every harmonic bong since she'd gone to bed. Her body was exhausted. Her mind, on the other hand, refused to stop its Ferris wheel whirl. Her emotions like the clock's pendulum swung from comfort to exasperation.

Not even the bubbly soak helped.

Gus's return had awakened everything she'd blocked. Things she thought she'd never feel again. She hadn't hesitated to fire when the gang member held that knife to his throat. No surprise she fainted. Then waking up in his arms had felt so right, so natural.

The pull and weight of his betrayal with Claudia had always been her shield. Tonight, she learned there had been nothing between him and Claudia except an undercover assignment.

He hadn't lied. He'd been doing his job. Did that make her renewed feelings okay? Would a relationship between them even work?

Her brief attempt to form a connection with Todd hadn't.

There'd been no spark. He was a kind man who deserved someone who could give him her whole heart. Mary-Dee knew she could never be that woman.

Because you'll always love Gus Nolan.

Throwing off the covers, she slid her feet into her slippers. Relationships never worked out for her. Not one with Gus. As long as he remained an agent, there'd be other undercover assignments. Her heart couldn't take the lies he'd have to tell her.

Yes, she'd forgive him this time. After all, he'd been trying to protect her.

She pulled her robe from the bedpost. Maybe a glass of warm milk with Quik like Aunt Nellie used to fix her would chase the thoughts of him away. It'd worked when he'd gone off with her sister and broken her heart.

If that didn't work, she'd watch a classic movie until she fell asleep. By breakfast, she'd have herself under control again.

He'd move on to another assignment once the MS-13 trial was over.

She'd go on with her life.

Descending the stairs, she noticed the outline of a truck under the trees out front. Her hand froze on the stair rail. Had more MS-13 goons been sent to watch her?

She patted her robe pocket. No phone. She'd left it on the bedside table. She debated going back to get it.

Too late. Whoever was out there knew she was inside. She shouldn't have turned the stairway light on.

She crept to the window on either side of the front door and peeked out to see a very familiar pickup. Gus gave a small wave and a silly smile.

She inhaled deeply, flew out the door, and banged on the truck window.

He rolled the glass down slowly. "Yes?"

"Why won't you accept I can take care of myself?"

"I'm only being your backup."

"Go home."

"Fine." He rolled the window up with a jerking motion. Anger sparked golden starbursts in his dark coffee-colored eyes, reminding her of other emotions she'd seen in his gaze, emotions she'd given into before when she'd been young and foolish.

She wouldn't be foolish again. She whipped around and stomped back inside.

Gus called the police station before he started the truck. "This is Agent Nolan. I need a patrol car at the Ross farm for surveillance. Right away."

Knowing she was watching from behind a curtain upstairs, he drove to the end of her road and killed the lights. She wouldn't be able to see him through the trees that lined her driveway. He waved when the patrol car arrived and went home.

The next morning as the first light of dawn filtered through his window, Gus's phone chimed. He rolled over and reached for it on the night table trying to get a grip. The phone slid onto the floor with a thud. The chime grew softer, muffled. He sat up to look for it. Dog's soft brown eyes met his. The phone dropped into his lap.

Dog slobber covered the screen. He picked it up with his thumb and pointer finger and rubbed the screen against his chest. He read through the drool.

Come have breakfast. I'm making scones.

Meena's scones were to die for. They'd been the reason he got up every morning when he'd come to live with her after his parents' sailboat went down in a Long Island Sound storm. But at this hour were they worth another hounding about why he'd bought the hunt cabinet, and why he and Mary-Dee weren't back together.

He hadn't had an answer when the estate service delivered the hunt cabinet, and he didn't have an answer this morning for either question. He'd acted on impulse when he'd bought the cabinet. Hadn't thought it through. Impulses had no explanation.

Why he wasn't back with Mary-Dee … that was complicated and simple. Until this smuggling mess was settled, there could be no answer.

On my way.

He pulled on jogging pants and a clean tee shirt. Dog pranced after him. More comfortable with him every day, same as he was getting used to having her around. The vet had confirmed Mary-Dee's prediction she was pregnant. Unfortunately, because she'd arrived on his doorstep pregnant, the doctor could only guesstimate how far along and when the puppies would come. If her size was any indication, Gus guessed it could be any day.

Meena greeted them at the screen door to the porch where she'd set the coffee carafe, and a bright yellow Fiesta platter loaded with scones on a wicker table. The scent of orange nearly brought him to his knees.

"Oh good. You brought her."

Meena disappeared inside and returned with the treat jar she kept. After having Dog sit, she offered a heart-shaped sweet potato treat, which was another reason Dog could be so fat. Meena constantly slipped her dog biscuits.

"The vet said not to feed her so many treats."

Meena fluttered her hand in the air. "What do they know? Carrying babies your body needs lots of nourishment. I should know. I looked like an elephant carrying your mother and felt like one too."

Gus sighed and poured himself a cup of coffee and reached for a scone. "These look delicious. Cranberry-orange?"

"Of course." Her cheeks rose and crinkled the corners

of her eyes. She sat across from him. Dog put her head on Meena's feet.

They ate and sipped in silence for a minute before Meena put her cup down. "We need to talk about ..." she leaned down and petted Dog's head, straightened and nailed him with a hard look. "a name for her. You can't keep calling her Dog. She needs a proper name."

"I told you I'm not keeping her."

"You just think you're not. You two have bonded. I shoulda let you have a dog when you were younger. Didn't want the added responsibility. I'm hands were full raising my grandson I thought. Big mistake. Now's a good time though. I betcha once those puppies come, you'll be wanting to keep all of 'em."

"Not happening. Not with my line of work. I could be called away at any time. A dog's not a practical pet for an FBI agent."

"Ah, but you see that's what makes it work this time. I'm here when you're not."

It was a hard argument to refute. He'd had zero luck finding a foster or rescue. No one wanted a pregnant dog. All offered to take the puppies once they came, but not the momma.

"I'll agree to naming her. What do you suggest?"

"She's yours so you need to come up with what suits you."

"Trouble?" he suggested.

Meena rolled her eyes. "I'm serious here. Needs to be soft, feminine. She's gonna be a momma."

"How about Lady as in *Lady and the Tramp* since she got herself knocked up?"

"I don't like your reasoning. All the same, it's a good name." Meena fluffed Dog's head. "I like it. Lady it is."

She offered Lady another treat then lifted her cup with both hands and took a sip. Her eyes zeroed on him. A hard conversation coming. He recognized the signs.

Gus lifted his heel, pushed back in his chair with his toes, and steeled himself for an inquisition.

"I saw Mary-Dee's car at your place late last night. What was that all about?"

"She brought me home after we gave our statements." He gave an abbreviated version of what happened at the covered bridge adding, "Stayed a while."

"And?" Meena smiled a matchmaker's smile.

He reached for another scone and took a bite. "And nothing. We talked. She left."

"I don't believe you'd let her go home alone after what happened at the covered bridge."

"I didn't. I followed her and parked outside in case another gang member showed up. Only she spotted me and stormed out to tell me to leave. I did but I called for one of Todd's patrol offices to watch her house."

"That's my boy. I don't like this mess. Not one bit."

Neither did he.

"I hear you. Between Todd and me, we got her covered even though she doesn't want us around. She thinks she can take care of herself. Shooting that guy before he sliced my throat has only boosted her confidence."

"Rightly so, but don't you two let her get by with it. MS-13 is not something to mess around with." And Meena didn't have any idea about the smuggling operation.

"We won't. One of us will be with her all the time."

She poured herself another coffee, added cream and sugar. "About that hunt cabinet. Why do you think she wouldn't accept it? She's always wanted one."

"I have no idea."

"What exactly did she say?"

"Too expensive. But that's just an excuse. She doesn't get to set a price limit on a gift."

"Her concern about cost is understandable. The girl's worked hard to keep that farm going and grow MDR Antiques. Money is something she thinks about."

He lifted his shoulders. "Maybe. More about accepting it from me, I'm guessing."

"You're going off with Claudia hit her pretty hard."

"Hit me hard too. I was in love with her, never Claudia."

"Don't you think it's about time you admit you still are? At least to yourself."

"Todd said the same thing."

"He's right. I think you carry those physical scars as well as the ones in your heart as a shield. That woman loves you. A grandmother knows these things. It's time you told her you love her too and you two start over."

Hadn't he said the same thing to Mary-Dee? Maybe it was time to act.

Meena's cuckoo clock bird bellowed seven *coo-coos,* and the couple popped out twirling to the music of some song he'd never figured out.

"I'll think about it. I need to get to MDR. Relieve the patrol car. Those two weren't the only gang members. MS-13 will be sending more. Mary-Dee's there rearranging the shop." He slapped his thigh for Lady to follow.

Meena stopped Lady. "She can spend the day with me."

Gus grinned. She was the one who should keep the dog. Lady spent as much time with her as him.

As he drove by on his way to MDR, Lady was lying at Meena's feet while she polished silver for her book club meeting.

A dog was probably a good thing for them both.

CHAPTER THIRTEEN

FROM HIS CAR hidden in the field behind a barn, Miguel watched the woman shouting at the man through his binoculars. He rubbed the back of his neck and rocked his shoulders up and down. They'd cut a pasture fence on the far side of Mary-Dee's land and followed a tractor path to a patch of land closer to the house.

Gordo lit another cigarette. The flame cast shadows on his bearded face. "We're wasting time watching her place. Gianna ain't here," he hissed in Spanish.

"Shut up and put that thing out. We don't want to be spotted."

Gordo crushed the cigarette against the dashboard and tossed the butt out the window. "Same thing happen to Marco gonna happen to us. We gonna go to jail I tell you."

The last thing Miguel needed was to be hauled in again. This time they'd lock him up and throw away the key.

"We're not stupid like Marco. We're not going to confront the bitch or the agent out there. Diablo says watch, we watch."

"What if the FBI gringo spots us." He motioned toward the truck parked in front of the house.

"Shut up. Not happening. Be patient. Gianna's either hiding in there or she will come."

If he could be the one who found her, he'd become Diablo's lieutenant. No more sitting in fields with locos like Gordo.

Miguel's phone vibrated like a rattlesnake in the console. He picked it up. "Hola."

His head nodded as he listened. "Si."

Tossing the phone onto the console, he whispered to Gordo, "We go now."

He inched the car toward the road between the pastures without headlights. Bushes and tall weeds scraped against the windows and doors. The car bounced as it hit potholes and rocks on the path that led to the main road.

"*Chingada madre*. I no see nothing. You're gonna hit something."

Pendejo. "I'm driving. I see fine."

"Turn on the low lights before you get hit something and get us killed."

"Moon's enough."

"Where are we going?"

"New orders."

The paved road appeared. Marco drove onto the farm road. With no streetlights or headlights, he still couldn't speed. Not on the narrow road with drainage ditches on both sides. Creeping along, he spotted the covered bridge.

He kept the car at a snail's pace across the clackety bridge, then flipped on the headlights at the highway intersection, turned, floored the accelerator, and sped down the highway.

CHAPTER FOURTEEN

KAYLEY ENGULFED HER in a smothering hug when Mary-Dee arrived at MDR on Monday morning. "OMG. I heard what happened. How are you? Should you even be here today? Go home. I can handle the shop."

"Stop. Gossip travels faster than the speed of light in Mount Pleasant." Mary-Dee squiggled out of the embrace as gracefully as she could. "I'm fine. I'd go crazy at home. I need to be here. Let me put my things away. We have a customer fast approaching." She gave a head nod toward the parking lot.

Kayley glanced out the glass door and stepped away "Sorry. It's just, I can't imagine. You rescued Gus. I want to hear all the deets."

"Later." Mary-Dee shoved her purse at Kayley and opened the door for the woman. "Welcome to MDR Antiques. Can I help you find something?"

"Please. My goddaughter is getting married, and I need a gift. She's always looking at my things. I thought you might have something."

"I think I know just the thing if you think she'd like Victoriana." Mary-Dee led her to a robin egg blue bride's basket in a sterling frame and explained the history of the Victorian-era wedding gift.

"Oh. It's lovely" The woman ran her fingers over the silver handle with the scrolls and flowers. "It's perfect. I'll take it."

Gus had come in while she was helping the woman. She watched Kayley touching his bandaged neck, gushing over him. It shouldn't bother her, but it did.

Why was he even here? The gang members following her had been arrested. Yesterday should have proved she could handle herself. A bodyguard wasn't necessary anymore. Time for her life to move on sans Gus Nolan.

After completing the transaction, she turned to him. "Why are you here? Didn't yesterday convince you I don't need a babysitter?"

"Those two weren't the only gang members out there. There'll be others. I have a job. I'm here until it's over. Get used to it."

His words carried threat and promise. Helplessly, she lifted her shoulders. "Fine, but it's a waste of your time and taxpayers' money." She whirled off to the coffee station to grab a cup of caffeine.

He followed.

Mary-Dee pressed her lips together tightly. After learning last night that he hadn't stopped loving her, the last thing she needed was having him around reminding her. She made her coffee in silence.

Kayley joined them and picked up a sugar cookie. "Okay, it's quiet again. Tell me all about yesterday. You really shot a guy, Mary-Dee?"

"She literally saved my neck." He gave a falsetto chuckle.

Kayley's eyes grew saucer sized. "For real? That's something out of a movie."

"Yes." Mary-Dee studied her coffee. It had been too real. "Gus disabled the one in the car, so it was a joint effort."

Gus circled his arm around Mary-Dee's shoulders. "We make a good team."

The feel of being tucked in his arm sent a full body rush through her. In the past, they'd been good together at work and in their private lives … before his assignment in Florida … with Claudia. Before he stabbed her in the heart. She side-stepped, not ready to go there again.

"We did, and yesterday should have proved I do not need you hanging around anymore."

"This is far from over. I'm not going anywhere."

The shop bell signaled another customer's arrival. Kayley dabbed the cookie crumbs from her lips. "I'll get that. Sounds like you two have a few things to sort out."

"We can walk over to that café across the parking lot. Have some privacy for a talk." Gus suggested when Kayley was out of earshot.

Her eyes shot darts at him. "There's nothing to talk about. What I need is for you to go away."

The shop bell rang again as two more customers entered.

"Go help them. I have paperwork to do." She walked away.

Gus stayed where he was, hands in his pockets, frowning after her. What she wanted and what she got were going to be two different things.

Once the flow of customers stopped, Gus went back to Mary-Dee's office. He tapped timidly on the doorframe. "It's turned slow. Todd called and invited us to join him at The Mill. You ready to cut out early? Let Kayley close."

"He called me, too. You can go on ahead. I've got to get these layaway invoices sent out today. Maybe after that."

"Let me help?"

"Not that many more."

"Then teamwork will make it go fast." He winked.

She exhaled a shallow breath and handed him a stack of envelopes. "Fine. Seal and stamp these. I hate that adhesive taste on the envelopes."

He wasn't fond of envelope glue either. He wouldn't complain, though, she was letting him help. That counted as progress. Setting the envelopes on top of the printer with his back to her, he read over each invoice.

Over the last few weeks, he'd come to agree with Todd that Mary-Dee was not personally a part of the smuggling operation. But antiques with the stolen objects were run through her shop. He needed hard evidence. The coming shipment of diamonds would provide that.

He tapped the stack of envelopes on the printer. "All done here. You ready? I'll follow you home then we can drive over to The Mill together."

Shaking her head, she pushed from her desk. "I'll meet you there. That way you and Todd can stay as long as you want. I can eat and head home."

He chose not to push. Win a few, lose a few. "I'll see you there."

Mary-Dee turned into The Mill parking area and dashed to the entrance. She didn't like being late. A rush of customers arrived as she was leaving MDR, and she stayed to help Kayley. She'd half expected the patrol car following her to turn on its lights and pull her over for speeding. He pulled in behind her and waited until she was at The Mill door before leaving.

She spotted Gus and Todd in deep conversation at a table outside on the patio. The set of Todd's shoulders told her whatever Gus was saying he didn't like. She waved off the hostess and made her way to the patio.

"We're not ready to –" Gus stopped when he spotted her. "You finally made it."

Todd stood and pulled out a chair for her. "Everything okay? You're late. That's not like you."

"Rush of customers as I was leaving. Sorry."

"You could have texted to let us know," Gus grumbled.

She raised her brows. "I'm sure the patrol car kept you informed."

"You're here now. It's fine." Todd took his seat again.

"What can I get you to drink?" The waitress handed her a menu. "I'll take your order when I bring your drink."

Mary-Dee gave her drink order and took the offered menu. "What aren't you ready for?"

They both gave her questioning looks. "When I walked up Gus was saying 'We're not ready'. Not ready for what?"

Gus brushed his hand in the air. "Not important."

Mary-Dee's iced tea arrived, and they placed their food orders. Todd raised his cider mug. "Outstanding job at the bridge, my friends."

"Thank you," she said with a smile. "But don't you think it's time you two told me what's really going on here? Gianna isn't a big fish. Neither am I. Whatever is going on isn't about protecting me."

"Nothing's going on," Gus answered.

"I thought dinner would be a good idea. The three of us haven't had a chance to catch up," Todd added.

Their answers sounded too pat, too rehearsed. Todd's eyes never met hers. His gaze went to the table and confirmed he was hiding something. She just didn't know what.

"I don't believe you. Nailing those mob members is important but doesn't call for an undercover operation. I worked at the bureau, remember." Her gaze nailed Gus. He gave a barely perceptible wince. "What's going on?"

Before he could reply, the waitress arrived with their food. Conversation shifted to casual topics and reminisces. Sharing a meal with two men she cared for eased the tension between her shoulders. The certainty that there was something else in play here didn't. She should let it rest. She couldn't. Wouldn't.

"When are you two going to tell me the real reason Gus is here?"

"We told you protecting you and finding Gianna so she can testify." Gus forked a shrimp and put it in his mouth.

"That's what you want me to think. I'm not stupid. I've watched you drilling Kayley, searching the shop, asking me questions about customers. There's something else."

"Your recent encounter with those MS-13 thugs should be proof that his presence is necessary," Todd said.

"Come on. I'm an ex-agent. There are dozens of witnesses for the dozens of trials involving MS-13. There's not enough manpower available for what you're saying is going on. Either you trust me, or you think I'm part of whatever you're doing. Which is it?"

Gus probed her from across the table. "I understand your suspicions. If our roles were switched, I'd be where you are. That doesn't mean I'm not doing exactly what I said I am."

"But with the trial starting, guarding me is a waste. Let Eric or someone find something else for you to do."

"He can't control that or this. We're not in charge. FBI is lead," Todd said.

"Okay then tell me what is going on."

Gus's face paled and he gave a heavy, fatalistic sigh. "Okay. Truth is, we're not at liberty to say."

Of course, they couldn't share. If her time with the Bureau taught her nothing else, information was always based on a need to know.

"Thank you for your honesty."

At least now, based more on what they hadn't said than what they had, she knew there was more to Gus's bodyguarding than waiting for Gianna to turn up.

CHAPTER FIFTEEN

SUNDAY AFTERNOON MARY-DEE took a leisurely walk to the covered bridge. She would not allow what happened there to spoil the special place. The morning sun cast strong rays on the bold yellow of wild buttercups and the three-note call of the sparrow filled the air. She scanned the puffy white clouds floating in the soft blue of the sky. The sight and sounds soothe her troubled spirit.

She sank onto the log by the river, pulled off her sneakers, and twirled her toe in the water letting the conversation from last night circle like the water around her foot. Gus and Todd's responses confirmed her suspicions. Protecting her from MS-13 was not the main reason for Gus's presence.

Not revealing his true assignment made sense too. She didn't like it, but she understood. Whatever the reason, it had to have something to do with her shop.

She arched her back and stretched side to side. She could figure it out. Hadn't she had the same training as them? Clearly, antiques were involved which meant there were two options — fakes and/or smuggling.

Gus had been extremely interested in Mr. Smyth and his purchases. Was Gus tracking him?

Smuggling, fakes, or Smyth, it could be either or all three. Which and exactly what, she didn't have enough information to be sure.

Nor could she figure out why they'd think she might be involved.

That they did stung. They'd known each other for years. She and Gus had once planned a life together. Now he thought she was a thief. The hurt melted into anger.

How dare they.

A tennis ball sailed over her shoulder and landed in the river sending a spray of water on her leg. A dog bolted past her into the water after the ball sending more water sprays her way. The dog she now recognized as Gus's dropped the ball at her feet and gave a body shake. She squeezed her eyes closed.

"I wouldn't have thrown it if I'd seen you. The tree hid you."

Opening her eyes she saw Gus slip his hand into his pocket and take out his handkerchief. Holding her face between his finger and thumb, he gently wiped at her cheeks.

"I'm so sorry." His head lowered, so close she could count his eyelashes, feel his breath on her lips.

He gave her a nanosecond to stop him before his lips lowered to hers. Firm at first then softening. A quick fleeting touch that sent her head spinning in a swirl of emotions.

Mary-Dee brushed his hands away.

"I won't apologize for that. I've been wanting to kiss you for a long time."

Lady nosed her head into Mary-Dee's lap as if apologizing for Gus's boldness or her wet head. Which, Mary-Dee couldn't be sure. She ruffled her head. She's skinny. She's had the puppies?"

"She did. Six. Four boys and two girls."

"Good girl." Mary-Dee placed a kiss on her head. "Where are your babies?"

"Meena's on babysitting duty. Poor Lady's been with those squiggly, always-hungry pups twenty-four-seven for days now. I thought she needed a break."

So like Gus to notice.

"You named her Lady?"

"Meena insisted I give her a name. I thought it suited."

"I bet I can guess why." She chuckled. "Lady and the Tramp." It had been his favorite childhood video. In high school, he'd insisted she watch it with him because she'd never seen it. He'd never admit it, but Gus identified with Tramp, considered himself a protector. Which was why the failure of the Florida mission had hit him hard according to Todd.

"You'd be right."

"Are you going to keep her?"

"Haven't decided yet. She's kinda growing on me, though." He dropped onto the log beside her. "Glad to see you here. I worried you wouldn't come back."

"I wasn't going to let MS-13 take this place from me." She shifted to face him. "I've been thinking about what you and Todd didn't say last night. The real reason you're here has to do with my shop, doesn't it? The MS-13 trial and Gianna just offered you a good cover."

With a shrug, he bent over and untied his tennis shoes, pulled off his socks, and wiggled his toes in the water. "I'd forgotten how good this feels. We should take a dip like we used to," he said ignoring the question in her comment.

"Don't try to divert me. You think you can't trust me with this assignment because you think I'm involved."

"Who says I don't trust you? I've always trusted you."

"Then why not tell me what's going on?"

"You know the answer to that."

She gave a frustrated grunt. "Then I *am* a person of interest."

"I didn't say that."

He didn't deny it either. "What about Mr. Smyth? You've asked a lot of questions about him."

He picked up the tennis ball and slipped it into his pocket "If you won't go for a swim, let's walk a bit on the edge. Surely, we can find something else to talk about."

"I will figure this out."

And that was what worried Gus. The less she knew the safer she was because these guys did not play nice. MS-13 or the smuggling gang.

Beware of going soft, he chided himself. He'd lost control in Florida, and Claudia ended up dead. That could not happen again.

He offered his hand. "You were always good at figuring out minute details in briefings."

Mary-Dee took a sharp, frustrated breath and let him pull her to her feet.

He didn't release her hand as he walked toward the bridge with Lady on one side, Mary-Dee on the other. Soft mud whooshed between his toes with each step sending little bubbles up. He didn't like the feeling.

Dirt and grit caked between his toes. Getting it all out before he put his shoes back on would be next to impossible. He preferred walking on the edge of ocean sand that swept out to sea with each wave, leaving his toes clean.

He knew Mary-Dee loved the feeling, wiggling her toes into the soft, muddy goo. And that was why he'd suggested the walk.

"Is Meena ready for book club?" she asked. "I bet she's baking and cooking like mad."

"The house smells like a bakery. First, she made peach crisp with cinnamon which filled the house with cinnamon and peaches. Then she decided the blackberry cobbler would be better. I think she's boiled at least five dozen eggs. Poor hens can't keep up."

"I offered to help prepare something. She wouldn't hear of it."

"No. This is her big show, and she loves every minute of it. Thankfully, she only hosts once a year."

"It has turned into a competition of sorts. Last month's host did a Hawaiian theme."

"I heard. And Meena thinks she has to top that."

They reached the covered bridge. Cigarette butts and beer cans dotted the space underneath. "Looks like it's still a favorite make-out spot. Too bad we didn't bring a blanket." He grinned.

Mary-Dee's cheeks turned pinkish. He could see a part of her, however unacknowledged, was remembering too.

She made a show of checking her watch. "It's getting late. I need to get back."

"Lady's puppies are probably getting hungry too. Time to go, Lady." Gus pulled the tennis ball from his pocket and tossed it toward the log where they'd been sitting. Lady chased after it.

With their shoes back on, they climbed the soft slope to the road. The walk was slow and easy. No talk of his work or their kiss, only recollections of other times they'd walked the same path gradually drifting into companionable silence.

When she spotted the Mount Pleasant patrol car by the field at the far edge of her farm, he could hear her teeth grind. Sam opened the door. "There's something here I think you should see, sir."

Gus motioned to Mary-Dee. "Wait here."

"I will not. It's my house, my land." She pushed ahead of him.

"Unless you drove your tractor through this, someone's been watching the house." Sam pointed to the downed fence rails and tracks to the side of a lean-to storage shed in the field.

Mary-Dee gasped. "I didn't even notice. Fence rails fall all the time, so I guess it didn't register."

They tromped through the field following the tire impressions.

"Vehicular, not farm equipment. We can check her security cameras for plates." Sam pointed to the tire tracks.

Gus looked back at the road. "Won't do any good. They avoided the cameras. See. The cameras focus on the entrance and around the house. Not these outbuildings." *Stupid mistake.* One he'd have to fix for her.

"There was no reason, too expensive. Who'd want to break into my shed or barn?" Mary-Dee read his mind.

"Whoever it was left in a hurry. They didn't stop to put the fence rails back, but maybe we can match tire tracks or get shoe prints. Or fingerprints. I'll call for forensics."

Gus pursed his lips. "Likely as not, they wore gloves. Did you call Todd, I mean the chief?"

"Yes, sir. He's on his way."

"I need to get Lady back to her puppies. You stay with Mary-Dee until he does, okay."

Sam nodded. Gus turned to Mary-Dee. Her jaw set. Anger and what he thought looked like a touch of fear lined her face. Good. The situation was finally sinking in. "I'll be right back." He slapped a come-along palm against his leg. "Come on Lady."

Goosebumps rose on Mary-Dee's arm. A strained sound filled her voice. "They were probably here all night ... watching."

"Yes, ma'am," Sam answered. "That's why we're gonna wait right here for backup. Someone could still be in there." He led her to his patrol car.

Minutes later, Gus returned and leaned against the car door. She rolled down the window. "That was fast."

"Lady and I jogged home. I drove my truck back. Anything happening here?"

"Todd and Sam are checking inside."

"I'll go check on them." He stepped toward her house.

The car door opened. "I'm coming too." She cocked him a look. "Don't argue."

When they entered the front door, Sam came down the stairs. "All clear upstairs."

"I see no signs down here that they have been inside. Must have been watching the house for Gianna to show up." Todd joined them. "It's safe now. Sam's gonna hang around just to be sure."

"I—"

Gus pointed his finger at her, shushing her. "You won't complain. Yes, you proved you could take care of yourself. I don't care. Sam stays with you, or I do." He gave her a half-smile, his dark eyes settled on her, firing her senses and filling her mind with a kaleidoscope of images and possibilities.

His earlier kiss and the crackling atmosphere between them rushed around in her head. She couldn't risk a repeat of that.

"Fine."

CHAPTER SIXTEEN

GUS DIDN'T GO to MDR on Monday, not because Mary-Dee insisted he stay away. Meena needed his help setting up her book club luncheon. Todd covered Mary-Dee and the shop with a patrol car in the parking lot which would follow her to his grandmother's where he'd take over.

He enjoyed the book club. Meena had made him the first male member of MPBPs (Mount Pleasant Book Posse) back in high school. Youngest and only male back then. Whenever he was in town at book club time, he'd participate. These days MPBP boasted a membership of men and women ranging in age from eighty-eight to sixteen, the granddaughter of a longtime member.

Meeting attendance varied with about a dozen showing up regularly on the first Monday of the month. Today Meena anticipated a full house. Always was whenever she hosted.

"More to the left," Meena instructed as he set up tables under the sprawling oak in her backyard. She spread each table with a vintage quilt that had grown too thin to be of use on a bed then added McCoy vases with pastel designs she'd filled with her roses in the center. Standing back, she surveyed the setup and smiled.

"Mary-Dee should be here any minute, and we can start arranging the serving table."

A car door slammed, punctuating her words. Mary-Dee rounded the house. "So sorry, last-minute customer."

Gus hustled to intercept her. "Please, don't mention our discussion about Claudia to Meena. She doesn't know the truth, yet."

"And why not?" Mary-Dee slapped her hands on her hips like a mother ready to scold a child.

Stalling, he glanced over her shoulder to see a man and his son heading down the path through Meena's yard to the river with their fishing gear.

They waved. He waved back.

Town folk had been cutting through Nolan property to fish along the bank of the Shenandoah for as long as Nolans had owned the land. Sometimes he'd go down and chat with them like his grandfather used to do. Not today. He had to stay close to keep Mary-Dee from mentioning Claudia to Meena before he did.

"Well," Mary-Dee drilled him.

"I've never told her I got shot and spent all that time in the hospital. She thinks I was on an assignment."

"You not coming to Claudia's funeral? I can't believe she'd buy that."

"I wanted to spare her. She worries too much at her age. Please don't say anything. Especially today. You know how important her turn hosting for book club is to her."

"You two finish your little tête-à-tête. We got work to do," Meena called from behind them.

"Please," he said softly and brushed Mary-Dee's hand. "I am going to tell her."

She pulled her hand to her side, dropped her chin in a tiny nod, and followed his grandmother. "What's next?"

For now, his secret was safe. He couldn't count on how long though. He'd need to come clean and soon.

Thirty minutes later, the buffet table was loaded. Beads of sweat gathered on the pitchers he filled with sweet tea and water at the tables. Mary-Dee helped Meena serve as guests began to arrive.

Gus piled his Limoges luncheon plate with six tuna fish and chicken salad sandwiches. He felt Meena's glare. He gave a sheepish grin. Who only ate one of those tiny triangles? They were hardly the size of a bite. He needed more sustenance. Adding a generous helping of sliced fruit salad next to the pile of sandwiches, he stepped out of line to find a seat and wait for others to join him. By the time the last guest was served, the only seat left was next to him.

The click of silverware on fine China soon filled the air as Meena took her seat at the head table.

"I didn't plan it," he defended the accusation in Mary-Dee's eyes when she dropped her plate beside him.

"Of course not." Sarcasm rang in her words. Sitting, she angled her body to her other side toward the silver-haired lady with a broad-brimmed straw hat. "What did you think about this month's book?"

The wrinkle-faced woman gave a smile that looked more like a grimace. "Truthfully, dear, I'm not sure I believe that girl could raise herself alone in a North Carolina marsh. Have you ever been in a marsh?"

Mary-Dee shook her head.

"Well, I have and it's not believable. A little girl surviving on her own in that? Not gonna happen."

"It's fiction, Ms. Louise, not fact. Ms. Owens makes it believable. Wouldn't you agree?" The mayor, sitting across from them, asked. With that question, the book discussion was off and running.

Mary-Dee's shoulders relaxed. So did Gus's.

"Dessert." Meena set her famous blackberry cobbler dessert on the serving table. Attendees formed a line to grab a dessert plate.

Gus felt a tap on his shoulders and turned to see the man who had gone down to the river. His young son with his face burrowed into his neck in his arms. His face was ashen. "Excuse me, sir."

Gus stepped out of the line and guided the pair away, out of earshot from the others. "Everything okay?"

"No, sir. I'm so sorry to interrupt your party," the fisherman answered. "I need to use your phone. There's been some kinda accident. A girl's laying on the bank."

He braced his chin on his son's head, cupped his ear, and mouthed, "I think she's dead."

"I'm an FBI agent. Wait here. I'll handle it." Gus went back to whisper in Mary-Dee's ear. "We have a situation."

"Excuse us please." He guided her aside. "There's a body by the river. You and Meena will need to keep everyone calm."

"Of course." Mary-Dee followed him back to the man and his son.

"Mary-Dee, this is…"

"Bobby," his father filled in

She smiled at the child. "Bobby, do you like puppies?"

He grinned displaying a gap between his top teeth. "Yes, ma'am."

"Mr. Gus's dog, Lady has six puppies I think you will love. Let's go check 'em out."

The father set him on his feet.

"You know where the key is, same place as always," Gus said.

Bobby took Mary-Dee's offered hand, and they moved away.

"Show me." Gus and the boy's father man climbed down the stone stairs toward the riverbank.

He motioned for the man to stand back as he examined the body. The river lapped gentle waves that lifted her hair from her face and back again. Young. Female. Shoes missing. Dress in shreds. Her arms were black and blue. Whether from the river's current or fighting for her life, he couldn't be sure. The bullet hole in her back most certainly had not come from the river. He pulled his cell from his pocket and called Todd.

The best access to the area was through Meena's backyard. He went back up the stairs with the fisherman to let his grandmother know her book club was about to become an active crime scene.

Meena greeted him at the top. "Is that what I think it is?" Her years as an FBI Bureau clerk kept her expression calm and her voice steady. She'd no doubt dealt with dozens of victim photos similar to the scene below.

Gus nodded. "Todd's on his way."

Meena's face blanched. "Can't it wait until we finish? We're almost done."

"Meena … you know that's not how this works. We need to get forensics down there as fast as possible."

She dipped her head. "Of course. That was selfish. I didn't mean …" She faced the fisherman. "I'm sorry. It must have been horrible for you and your son. Come inside. I'll get you some iced tea. Maybe some cobbler if you'd like."

"Good idea." Gus circled her shoulders and squeezed. "Todd will be unobtrusive, no sirens. He's gonna need to question everyone about whether they saw or heard anything. Don't let anyone leave."

Her cheeks puffed until Gus thought she'd explode. She took a deep breath. "Fine. But do not bring that body bag through here in front of my guests."

"I'm sure they'll be discreet."

CHAPTER SEVENTEEN

By DARK, THE emergency vehicles were gone. The fisherman, his son, and all the guests were sent home with the caution to contact Todd if they remembered anything else. Todd lingered. He sat next to Mary-Dee and took her hands in his. His voice was soft in the avuncular tone she realized he used to calm nerves.

"The coroner will get a positive ID but my guess is it's Gianna. I'm sorry. I know you wanted her to be safe."

True, but she wasn't naïve.

"The odds were against Gianna once she went out on her own. She should never have left the safe house. I was hoping for a miracle. What happens with the trial now?"

"The lawyers decide if they have enough to go ahead without her testimony. We'll focus on finding her killer and go after the two for their attack on you and Gus."

"Hardly seems fair that the drug dealer who originally beat Gianna gets off," Meena said.

"Fair is not a word we use very often in this business. The law rules." Exasperation threaded Gus's words.

Mary-Dee nodded. The rule of law was a contributing factor to her departure from the Bureau. All an agent's hard work could so easily be cast aside in court over a technicality. Some obscure something they never knew existed. All the hard work cast aside as the bad guy walked.

"Sad but true. I'll head back to the station now. Wait for the ME report." Todd hugged Mary-Dee, then Meena. "I'm so sorry your book club meeting was spoiled."

"Wasn't your fault. Just find whoever killed that girl," Meena said.

"We will. Gus, can I have a word?" The two went outside.

Meena plopped into her favorite reading chair with a heavy sigh. "We never even got around to the book question discussions. What an afternoon!"

"One I'm not interested in repeating anytime soon. I'm going to head home," she said.

"Don't you want to wait and let Gus go with you, just in case?"

"Absolutely not. The only good to come from all this is Gus doesn't have an excuse to be hanging around me all the time anymore."

"You don't mean that." Meena gave a slow wink. "Be careful going home. This isn't over yet."

Todd paused at his car. "You realize we just lost your cover for being at MDR with Mary-Dee."

Gus shifted his weight from foot to foot. "Blowing my cover seems to be my latest modus operandi."

"This was no more your fault than what happened with Claudia. You'll need another cover, or we have to tell Mary-Dee the truth. I vote for telling her. I refuse to believe she's involved with the smuggling. Her shop, maybe, but I've seen no evidence she's aware of what's going on. Have you?"

"No. But her shop *is* being used as the smuggler's dump site, either she or Kayley has to be involved."

"She's not. I'd stake my life on it. My money's on Kayley."

"All I know for sure is pressure's building. Customs holding the container with the diamonds was not part of the plan. The smuggler is getting antsy and him being antsy is never good. The lid's going to blow soon."

"Yeah, with Mary-Dee sitting on a powder keg." Todd opened his car door. "She knows there's no real reason for you to be around. I suggest you use the thing you have for her to keep her safe."

"I do not have a thing. Those feelings died in Florida." *Liar.*

"You're only fooling yourself. After all these years, I know when you're getting a thing." Todd slid behind the wheel. "The truth is going to come out and bite you on the butt. This time she may not forgive you."

"Don't I know it?"

Lying to thieves and murderers was one thing. Lying to the two women he loved was a whole other dilemma.

Mary-Dee waved as she drove by. "You got her covered?"

Todd gave a nod. "On it. I'll send Sam."

Once inside, Gus plopped on the sofa opposite Meena. "We need to talk."

"Maybe later. It's been a long, stressful afternoon. I'm not the spring chicken I used to be. I'm going to take a long bath and head to bed with a good book."

His grandmother had to be exhausted. He was.

"Sure. I'll go take care of Lady. Then make a run over to Mary-Dee's. Be sure Todd's got a patrol there."

Gus didn't need an ME report. He was positive the body was Gianna. With their main witness dead, MS-13 should be out of the picture. The smuggling gang had no reason to watch Mary-Dee's house.

Still. Better to check.

"That's a great idea. Maybe go inside and talk to her." With a wink, Meena headed upstairs.

When he got to Mary-Dee's farm, he found her and Sam lifting the split rails of the fence back into place. He reached for the end she held.

She shoved him away. "I got it." She stomped her foot on the rung forcing it into the slot. "When will you get it through that thick skull of yours that I don't need you to do things for me."

He raised both hands in surrender. "My bad. I just came by to check how you are after this afternoon."

"I'm fine. It's over. Neither of you need to come to MDR tomorrow. The threat is gone." She stuffed her work gloves in her back jeans pocket and marched to the kitchen door.

"What was that all about?"

"Too much drama for Mary-Dee's quiet orderly world."

Sam shook his head. "Women. I'll never figure 'em out."

He patted Sam's shoulders. "Don't even try."

CHAPTER EIGHTEEN

FOR TWO DAYS Gus played with the puppies and drove by MDR repeatedly, staying out of sight. On the third day, his cell rang. "Yes, sir."

He ended the call and slid the phone back into his pocket, herded the puppies into the area he cordoned off for Lady and her brood. After changing into a shirt that didn't have puppy drool, he called Todd to let him know he was on the way.

He gave a nod to the desk clerk and headed to Todd's office. "Customs is releasing the shipment. It's being repacked and shipped to Joe Majors' Auction."

"Ever figure out why it was held up to begin with?"

"Crazy thing. A young, overzealous customs agent spotted a sextant on the list. Unfamiliar with the term, he flagged the container and searched the entire shipment trying to be sure it wasn't code for sex trafficking."

Todd rolled his eyes. "He must not have had a naval background, or he would have recognized what a sextant is."

"Exactly and because he didn't, we're on hold until Majors has the container inventoried and sets an auction date. I suspect that will be done fairly quickly. He lost business while the shipment was detained."

"Nothing for us to do until the auction is announced. Have you told Mary-Dee?"

Gus shook his head. "I don't want her tipping off Kayley or our smuggler. Best she doesn't have any idea."

"Your call."

"Yes, and I hope it's the right one. She and Kayley are so close I can't risk her giving away the plan. We'll have agents at the auction whenever Majors schedules it, and we let it play out like any other auction. Only we'll all be watching the desk and who bids on it."

"You think Kayley will."

"I do, proxy for our smuggler. If the pattern holds, she'll buy the desk, have it delivered to MDR, and then the smuggler will come buy it, remove the diamonds, and drop the desk at a different auction house somewhere in the Route 50 area."

"Slick plan."

"It is except he picked Mary-Dee's shop. We're gonna nail him this time."

"I feel a little sorry for Kayley. She's been duped as much as Mary-Dee."

"Not true. Kayley chose to cooperate, work for him. Mary-Dee didn't."

"Does that mean you agree Mary-Dee is not involved?"

"I'm giving her the benefit of the doubt. Kayley, not so much."

"We still have no idea what the smuggler looks like."

Gus pushed forward in his chair and set his laptop on the corner of Todd's desk. "The analysts have come up with a composite of his aliases. He's crafty and has dozens of personas he can use. I'm convinced one is Mr. Smyth, Mary-Dee's client who visits periodically on his way to D.C. Probably uses a different persona with Kayley."

He pulled up an AI mug shot of Mr. Smyth.

"Has Mary-Dee seen this?"

"No. The less she knows the better. An agent at the last auction snapped this picture of Kayley talking to this man. Program came up with this." He pointed to the image on the screen. "Same shaped eyes, different hairstyle, color, and lots more facial hair. I'd stake my life he's Smyth with molded stage makeup to raise his cheeks."

Todd studied the two photos. "I guess it could be."

"It is. Look what our analyst did." A series of faces morphed from auction man to Mr. Smyth.

"Amazing what technology can do these days."

"He's our man. We just don't know what he will look like this time. We'll zero in on anyone bidding on the desk."

"Will Mary-Dee go?"

Gus raised his shoulders in a shrug. "Who knows? She's never liked auctions so probably not. We'll wait and see."

Later that afternoon Gus waltzed into MDR Antiques like he belonged. "How's it going?"

Mary-Dee rolled her eyes. "Why are you here?"

"Can't I come and visit with you and Kayley?"

"Works for me," Kayley said with a flirtatious flutter of her eyelashes.

Mary-Dee's phone rang. She answered and walked away, returning minutes later. "That was your Aunt Darlene. Joe Major's truck just left to pick up the container from customs."

"Hooray! At last." Kayley clapped her hands. "Guess I know what I'll be doing as soon as they get it all inventoried." Her phone pinged. She checked the message and went to the storeroom.

Mary-Dee turned to Gus. "Did you know?"

"I do now." Gus gave a closed-mouth smile. "Are you going?"

"Not planning on it. That's where Kayley excels."

"But you have to admit you enjoy a good bidding war and those hot dogs."

She smiled, a smile that lit her eyes. "I do. We'll have to see when the auction gets scheduled."

Monday of the next week, word came that the auction was set for Friday night. Mary-Dee did not go. On advice he might be recognized from the other botched undercover, Gus didn't go to the auction even though he wanted to, other agents would be there.

At eleven pm, Todd called. "The cheese is in the mousetrap. Played out the way we predicted. Kayley bought the desk and several other furniture pieces."

"Thanks for the heads up. Now we wait."

———

Gus gave a thumbs up to Kayley when he walked into MDR Antiques the next morning. "Congratulations. I heard you made quite the haul."

"And exactly how did you hear about Kayley's *haul?*" Mary-Dee asked frostily.

"Aunt Darlene does work at the auction house. She called Meena before breakfast and told her about Kayley's purchases. Said delivery would be today. Meena sent me to help unload and rearrange." He flashed his most convincing smile. The frown on Mary-Dee's face said she wasn't buying it.

"Go home. Major's guys help unload. Kayley and I can handle the shop rearranging ourselves."

"Enough arguing, you two. Truck's here." Kayley pointed to the parking lot.

Major's Auction delivery truck was backing up to the shop door.

Mary-Dee clapped her hands. "After all the bad stuff lately, I need some good news. I can't wait to see what you got."

Gus propped the front door open. "Me either."

The first piece off the truck was a tapestry loveseat. Not something he would've wanted, but then he wasn't in the business of selling. Hopefully one of Mary-Dee's customers would love it.

Next came a pine plank kitchen table. He could see that in a farmhouse. Even his barndominium.

A lamp table and washstand followed.

Lastly, the two men lifted a black cottage desk off the truck. The drop-down front had a silhouette inlaid of a Victorian woman and flower clusters painted around the glass doors of the hutch top with intricately turned finials.

And somewhere inside a bag of diamonds worth half a million dollars.

"Stop. That's going home with me. Put it in the back of my SUV."

Gus's heart stuttered. "What?"

"I love it." Mary-Dee beamed.

The hairs on the back of Gus's neck prickled. Tension he could almost smell filled the air. The last thing he needed was the goods at Mary-Dee's house.

"I know you're looking for a writing desk but …" Kayley's pupils grew large. "this is so not your style. You're natural wood, oak, and walnut. More formal, not cottage painted."

"But look at that silhouette of a lady. It's perfect." She pushed the key fob to raise her SUV's hatch. "Will you grab a couple of our furniture blankets from the back?"

Kayley went inside and returned with the double-sided furniture blankets. Mary-Dee smiled as she wrapped the desk. Kayley's hands tremored. They stepped away and watched the two delivery men lift the small desk into her SUV.

Happiness glowed in Mary-Dee's eyes. She hugged Kayley's stiff body. "I love it. Thank you."

The subtle undercurrents made Gus uncomfortable. He moved next to Kayley. A faint line of sweat beaded on her brow below the bright-colored bandana holding the mop of springy curls off her face. "Everything okay?"

"Yeah. Surprised that's all." She whirled and went inside.

Mary-Dee tipped the deliverymen then locked her SUV. "Don't you have someplace you need to be?"

"Nah. I'll hang around here, help with moving the heavy pieces for you. And then follow you home and help you unload your new desk." He leaned forward and gave her a peck of a kiss on the nose.

"I give up. Do what you want." She stomped inside, shaking her head.

CHAPTER NINETEEN

MEENA'S LINCOLN TOWN Car sat in front of her house when Mary-Dee arrived after she closed the shop. She backed her SUV beside it. Gus pulled his truck on the other side.

"Before you ask, Darlene went to check out your new stuff. Kayley told her you'd taken a desk home. Darlene called me. I had to come see it."

"The FBI could take lessons from your communication network." Gus joined Mary-Dee at the back of her SUV. "Get the door for us."

After they got the desk inside, Gus moved it around Mary-Dee's den at least a dozen times. Finally, Meena suggested, "I think I remember Nellie had a small desk in that corner."

Mary-Dee gave a nod. "You're right."

"You're sure?" Gus said after he positioned the desk in the corner.

Meena and Mary-Dee held thumbs up high.

"Great. Before one of you changes your mind again, can we go have the chicken and dumplings Meena brought? That aroma has been calling me ever since we got here." Gus raised his arm in a come-along wave.

Mary-Dee led the way.

"You've redone the kitchen," Gus said.

"No choice. Aunt Nellie's old beige and green porcelain stove gave up the ghost. That started a domino effect that led to new counters and cabinets and the porcelain farm sink."

"She did good, didn't she? Kept the feel of the old with all the modern," Meena said.

"She sure did. How can I help?" he asked.

"Set the table. Placemats are in that drawer and silverware there."

"How about a salad to go with the dumplings?" Mary-Dee opened the side-by-side stainless refrigerator.

"Sounds wonderful." Meena lifted a large tomato from the pottery bowl on the counter. "Are these from your greenhouse?"

Nodding, she slammed the iceberg lettuce head against the counter and began ripping leaves. "I grow them in there even though they could be outside now. Squirrels and birds aren't happy, but I have fresh tomatoes."

Meena pulled a chair from the pine harvest table in the center of the kitchen. "I'll sit and watch this domestic partnership. I like it."

Mary-Dee looked over her shoulder and frowned.

Gus gave an eye roll shrug.

As they ate, dinner conversation revolved around mundane, safe topics. Memories of meals shared in their younger days drifted in Mary-Dee's head. Her, Claudia, and Gus jabbering about the latest gossip at school while Meena and Aunt Nellie argued politics. She lifted her fork to her mouth and chanced a glance at Gus. He studied his dumplings. A faint smile curved his lips. He remembered too.

"There's leftover blackberry cobbler from book club. Brought it too. Over there by the crockpot.' Meena stood. "Three bowls?" At the affirmative nods, Meena filled bowls.

"Delicious, Meena." Mary-Dee's spoon scraped around her bowl to get the last of the cobbler. "Thank you so much for the dinner."

"We all needed a quiet evening. Between the dead body at book club and that awful scene at the cover bridge, it's been a rough few weeks. I haven't even had a chance to thank you for saving my grandson's neck and convincing him to come clean with me about Claudia."

"You told her everything?" Mary-Dee tilted her head, giving Gus a speculative look.

Gus pushed back in his chair. "Yeah. I did. You were right I should have told both of you sooner."

"Hold on," Meena said. "As long as we're making confessions, I might as well fess up too. I already knew."

Gus frowned. "How?"

"It wasn't Todd if that's what you're thinking. He kept your secret. I refused to believe an assignment would keep you from Claudia's funeral. It had to be something else. My friend at the bureau did a little checking for me and discovered you were at Walter Reed. It was hard not to rush up there to sit at your bedside." Meena swiped at her eyes with her napkin. "I understood why you didn't want me to know so I waited. I didn't like it, but I knew you'd come home, and my friend kept me posted on your progress."

"At least now everything's out in the open," Mary-Dee said.

Gus disguised a wince by folding his napkin. She'd never forgive him for what he was doing if he didn't tell her soon.

"I'm so sorry I blamed Claudia, and you by default, for what happened to my boy. I shouldn't have. Gus convinced me when he came home. That's why I went to Darlene's estate sale hoping to see you." She reached across the table and squeezed Mary-Dee's hand. "Please forgive me?"

Mary-Dee returned the squeeze. "Of course. Secrets can destroy everything good. Sometimes they can be necessary."

"Exactly. Undercover work is smoke and mirrors and lies. Sometimes subterfuge is what it takes to get the bad guy. Not that, it's an excuse for not telling both of you the truth about what happened in Florida." He looked from Meena to Mary-Dee.

"I know. Another one of those things I didn't like about my Bureau job." Mary-Dee gathered empty plates. "Let's get this cleaned up."

"Why don't you clean up, Gus? Mary-Dee and I'll go back to your place to check on Lady and the puppies. You could take her back home." Her eyes on Gus, Meena flashed a cagey little smile.

More matchmaking. Meena was determined to get the two of them back together.

"I'd love to see the puppies. Bet they've grown. I haven't seen them since book club."

"Works for me." Gus opened the dishwasher and mouthed a thank you to Meena. "I'll meet you there."

As Meena's car pulled onto the road, Gus pulled out his cell and called Todd. "We have a big problem."

"What now?"

"Mary-Dee brought the smuggler's desk home."

"She what?"

"Evidently, she's been looking for a small desk. She fell in love with this one when she saw it and loaded it directly into her car to bring home. It's in her den right now with a half million dollars in diamonds that she has no idea about inside. We need to double surveillance here starting now."

"I'll send Sam. We should also read Mary-Dee in. She needs to know what's going on."

"I can't do that without Eric's okay."

"Then get it because, with or without permission, I'm telling her first thing tomorrow morning. That desk in her home puts her life at risk."

"Don't you think I know that? I'm calling Eric next. If he says no, I'm with you. We're telling her anyway."

CHAPTER TWENTY

Hugo's phone jarred him from a deep sleep. He rubbed his eyes to read the caller ID. Seeing the name, cold, nauseous sweat pearled on his forehead. Afraid to answer, more afraid not to, he pushed to a sitting position on full alert.

"Yes."

"The shipment went to auction two days ago. Where are my diamonds?" the familiar voice asked.

Weakness would never be tolerated. He swallowed the tremor in his voice. "The piece was delivered to the antique shop as we planned. I'm going today to collect it."

"It's not there." The voice was soft, icy.

A flutter of panic rose in Hugo's throat. "It has to be. Those were the instructions. Same as always."

"It's not. You will clear this up at once. Our buyer is impatient." The pause was slight. "You do understand the penalty for mistakes."

"Yes." Hugo squeezed his eyes close. "I'll find your desk. Get the diamonds delivered."

He reached for a cigarette, lit it, and inhaled deeply, praying he spoke the truth.

"Our buyer is anxious." A sigh sounding like a hiss breathed through the phone. "You've done very well. Don't fail this time. I'd hate to lose you."

The phone went silent.

Hugo sat on the edge of the bed, clenched his fists, and took another puff. What could have happened? Kayley bought the desk, and he saw her make the arrangements for delivery to MDR Antiques. He'd planned to go there when they opened today to buy it.

He scrolled through his contacts until he found Kayley. "What's happened to my desk?"

"I know how much you wanted that little desk. Unfortunately, when they delivered it to the shop, the owner saw it and took it home. There was nothing I could do."

Fear like an icy shard stabbed his chest. That could not be.

He took slow even breaths. The pain eased. He had to think. The girl had no idea why he wanted the desk or what he'd been doing with the purchases she'd made for him this last year.

He had to get to the desk and the diamonds. The consequences were too dire.

Finally, he found his voice. "She has great taste." He faked a chuckle. "I'll have to keep my eye out for another one."

"We have a rolltop and a partner's desk at the shop. If either of those would work, I could get you a decent price."

"Afraid not. My space is small. Thanks anyway."

"I'm so sorry."

Anger and frustration simmered. She'd be more than sorry if he couldn't get to the diamonds.

So would he.

He tossed the phone to the bed and crushed the cigarette to tobacco crumbs. He'd quit breaking and entering jobs years ago. He'd have to polish up his old tools and come up with a plan. Fast.

CHAPTER TWENTY-ONE

NEXT MORNING GUS knocked on Mary-Dee's door shortly after sunup. Tension flowed through his body matching the steam from the cups in the cardboard container he held in his hand. "She is not going to like this."

"We should have told her from the beginning," Todd said in an I-told-you-so tone.

The door opened and Mary-Dee's eyebrows rose to her hairline. "What do you two want this early?"

"We'll explain." Gus pushed past her and headed to the kitchen.

"We brought doughnuts and coffee." Todd shook the white bag and followed Gus. He slid a kitchen chair out for her. "Have a seat."

"What is going on?" She made no move to sit.

Todd placed his hand on her shoulder and gave her a gentle push into the chair. "You should sit. We need to talk. You need to listen."

Gus pulled plates from her cabinet and put a glazed doughnut in front of her. "You might want a doughnut."

"I don't want a doughnut." She pushed the plate away. "I want to know what's going on. Out with it."

Gus sat across from her. "I'm on an undercover assignment."

"I knew it!"

"Stolen goods from Europe are being stashed in antique furniture and then put in containers and shipped to auction houses along the eastern coast. Pieces containing stolen objects are purchased by pickers for local shops – MDR Antiques is one of those shops." He waited for that piece of information to be absorbed then continued. "The smuggler – using various disguises – goes to the shop where the picker works, buys the piece, removes the contraband, and resells the antique at a different auction house."

Mary-Dee's mouth dropped, but she didn't speak. She simply stared at him as though he'd lost his mind. "You, MDR, and Kayley are under observation. Will be until the smuggler is in custody."

"I don't believe you." Her voice shook.

"It's true," Todd said.

"No. It's ridiculous. Do you really think something like that could go on in my shop and me not know it?" Her gaze went from Todd to Gus and back. She sucked in a shallow breath. "You think I'm in on it?"

"No," he and Todd said together.

Gus reached across and took her hand. "Never us. Eric and his superiors, on the other hand, had to be convinced. We're all in agreement now. You're not involved, but your shop is. Pieces containing stolen objects have been traced through MDR."

She pulled her hand from his. "How do you know?"

"I've gone through your inventory books and found pieces known to hold stolen items in the shop or on sales receipts."

"This is the real reason you came back. It was never about protecting me from MS-13."

"Not true," Todd said. "The situation with the MS-13 trial

did make the perfect cover for Gus. But never doubt we were protecting you. Still will until that trial is over."

"Especially now," Gus added.

"What do you mean especially now?"

"The desk that Kayley bought from Majors' auction—and you brought home yesterday—holds half a million dollars worth of stolen diamonds," Todd answered when Gus struggled to form the words.

Mary-Dee blinked then inhaled a deep breath and shoved from the table. She went to the cabinet, jerked out a mug, and returned to the table. She poured hot coffee from the paper cup, took a sip, and sat silent for a minute.

A half million dollars in diamonds in her desk. The possibility was too preponderous. It was madness.

Her shop tangled in international smuggling, not possible. A mistake.

Gus, Todd, The FBI, and the others were all wrong.

"You think my desk has stolen diamonds in it?"

Gus's eyes never left her. "We know. Our partners in Europe watched them being placed there, and you can bet the smuggler will be coming for his diamonds."

Slowly realization dawned. "You think Kayley's part of it."

Todd and Gus gave small, slow nods.

Mary-Dee lifted her chin. "Not Kayley. I don't believe you. She's not just my employee, she's my friend. I trust her."

That couldn't be. No, not her Kayley. Incredulity morphed into anger. "I won't have you accusing her."

"It's not an accusation. It's fact. She *is* buying pieces with stolen goods for them. The desk is not the first piece. We have a full list if you want to see." Gus' voice softened. "I know it's not what you want to hear."

The fire in Mary-Dee's eyes misted with tears. "She's worked for me for years. I never had reason to suspect."

"No one did." Todd patted her hand. "Not until Gus did his snooping."

"Why would she do that?"

"Money. For drugs, maybe. Her brother's an addict. Her mother's diabetes medicine maybe. It is expensive." Gus sipped his coffee. It wasn't his place to tell her that her friend had a gambling problem. "Once we question her, we'll know for sure."

"Are you going to arrest her?"

"Not today. We don't want to tip the smuggler we're on to him." Gus reached for her arm. This time she let him, his touch comforting. "It's important that you don't let on either. If you can't do that, you need to stay home until we catch this guy. Meena can fill in for you at the shop."

"Not necessary. I'll be fine." She could do it. She'd hate it, but she'd get the job done.

"The other concern is the smuggler needs to move quickly to get his diamonds. His buyer has had to wait because of that customs goof-up. That's made him impatient," Todd said.

"Fine. I'll take the desk back to the shop. He can have it and the diamonds."

"It's not that simple. The plan is to catch him in the act. This guy has slipped away from us before." Gus's shoulder rose as determination filled his voice and his eyes. "The FBI, Interpol, and local police agencies won't let it happen again.

"He won't come here if we're here," Mary-Dee insisted.

"Who knows what he'll do or force Kayley to do? As Gus says, he's desperate now. Gus is going to hang close. Get used to it," Todd said.

"Is it possible Kayley didn't know what she was doing? The smuggler was playing her?" Hope brightened Mary-Dee's face.

Gus took her plate to the sink. "Not likely, but possible."

She braced her elbows on the table and rubbed her eyes, hoping in vain to stop the tears. "This is a nightmare."

"Not if we catch the smuggler and get an evil man off the streets. You and Gus will be heroes," Todd said in his official reassuring tone used with suspects while she did her sketching.

She didn't want to be a hero. She'd left the Bureau to escape the drama, the violence, and here she was back in the middle of it. Her quiet life blown out of the water.

"What's the plan?" The thought of the smuggler coming into her home was too much. "I won't have some thief breaking into my house."

To her complete surprise, Gus moved in, cupped her chin. "I'll be staying in your guest room until we've got him. Agents in the fields. We spot him, they'll be here. I won't let anything happen to you."

"Between the Mount Pleasant force and the Bureau, you'll be covered twenty-four seven. But Kayley mustn't sense we're on to her. You have to act as if nothing has changed." Todd paused, "And when you're at the shop today, you'll let Kayley know how wonderful the desk looks in the den. Can you do that?"

Mary-Dee squared her shoulders. "Do I have a choice?"

Gus left to let Meena know what was going on and pick up some things. Todd stayed with her. She didn't argue. It was pointless. "How long do you think it'll take for them to figure out where the desk is?"

"I suspect they already know."

"You think Kayley called them?"

"Honestly, Mary-Dee, I don't know. I'd like to think she's not that deeply involved, but I've been in policework long enough to know better than to second guess. I know for sure they'll find you and come after the desk. That's why it's important that Gus be here with you."

"I do understand. We were a good team before he hooked up with Claudia."

Todd inhaled deeply, exhaled slowly. "You know that was an act for the assignment."

"So he says."

"Trust me. He hasn't ever stopped caring for you."

She tilted her head and lifted her shoulders in a shrug. "It's the truth and you still have feelings for him. Don't deny it."

That was the reason the two of them being together twenty-four hours a day was so not a good idea.

"As long as he's an agent, there can't be anything. I won't live with that uncertainty every day." She grabbed his mug and went to the sink.

"He hasn't told you?"

"Told me what?" She loaded the dishwasher.

"This is likely his last assignment. The higher ups weren't happy with the Florida situation."

"No, he hasn't. More lies." Another reason why she wouldn't let him back into her life. He wasn't honest with her.

"Not a lie," Gus came through the kitchen door. "Everything rests on how this all plays out."

She studied his face, his eyes that wouldn't meet hers. There was more he wasn't telling.

"I'll take my stuff up to the guestroom then we can head to the shop."

Mary-Dee pinned Todd with a questioning look. He returned a genuinely contrite shrug. "Not my story to tell. I'm off to start my day. Be safe." He disappeared out the door.

Upstairs getting ready herself, she could hear Gus shuffling around across the hall in the guestroom. Her hand shook as she put on her eyelash liner. This wasn't going to be easy.

And not because of the diamonds.

CHAPTER TWENTY-TWO

MARY-DEE HESITATED WHEN Gus opened the truck door for her in the shopping center parking lot. Her gaze drifted to MDR with the striped awnings she'd painted on the front windows to block the afternoon sun. On either side of the door, she'd placed large blue ceramic pots overflowing with petunias, begonias, and marigolds she'd planted. Wooden benches sat beside the pots. A spot for weary husbands to occupy while their wives shopped.

She'd worked so hard to make her shop welcoming, a success. She'd believed she left behind all the staring around every corner, watching her back.

Blood and violence. Lies and murder.

Or so she'd thought. She sighed deeply. The storefront blurred. She'd thought wrong.

"Mary-Dee."

"Huh?

"You coming?"

"Yes." She blinked away the tears, unsnapped her seatbelt, and slid out. Missing the running board, she fell forward straight into Gus's chest.

"Easy there."

He drew her so close his heart hammered against hers and his arms stayed around her a bit longer than necessary. She rested her forehead on his chest, welcoming his strength. "I'm not sure I can do this."

"Sure. You can." He rubbed his chin across the top of her head.

"Ah-ha." Kayley's voice came from behind them. "About time you two acted on what I've seen coming for a long time."

Mary-Dee stiffened. Gus twirled her around and slid his arm across her shoulders, tucking her into his side. "Took me a little time to convince the lady."

"I'm glad you did." Kayley walked on ahead. "I got the door."

"I'm never going to be able to pull this off," Mary-Dee whispered. "I can't even look at her."

"You'll do fine. I'll be right here with you." As much as she didn't want to find that comforting, she did.

The morning crawled even though customer traffic was above average for a weekday morning, with many making purchases including furniture pieces. She hated feeling so on guard with Kayley. It wasn't right to be alienated from the one person who had stuck beside her.

Waiting, watching for Kayley to make a mistake, to incriminate herself.

Or worse accidentally giveaway that she knew what Kayley had done. Made her heart hurt.

Gus was busy talking with a customer about an armoire. Kayley opened a jewelry case for another. Mary-Dee needed caffeine and sugar. She headed to the coffee and cookies.

Kayley followed her when she finished with her customer. "So, when did Gus move in? I want all the deets."

"Move in?"

"You arrived together in his truck. He was kissing you. I assumed you woke up together."

Mary-Dee coughed as her bite of cookie went down the wrong way. "He did not!" She took another sip of coffee to clear her throat.

"He's not living with you?"

Gus joined them, saving her from answering with a lie. "Where are all these people coming from?"

"I think I know. Wait right here." Kayley went to the office and returned with the Mount Pleasant Reporter. She held the newspaper up for them to read the headline, "Grim Find Disrupts Book Club."

"I figure they're all coming to gawk. The article should count as free advertising since so many are making purchases. The article mentions Meena, the book club, the father and son, and even named Mary-Dee as a local antiques dealer and book club member who knew the victim."

"The official ID on the body isn't even in. Who wrote this?" Mary-Dee jerked the paper from her hand.

"Yep. Eleanor." Eleanor Whitehall, a book club member and the biggest gossip of her high school class wrote for the Reporter. With all the details, she had to be the one. "I'm going to call her."

"Hold it." Gus stopped her.

The shop bell jingled. "I'll get it." Kayley went to greet the man.

"I'll call Todd and point out the obvious, have him give them a statement. He'll set the record straight." Gus pulled his cell from his pocket and walked away.

He returned shaking his head. "Todd's calling, but he thinks a retraction may be too late. Any MS-13 gang member who sees the article will be reminded that you knew Gianna and possibly think *she knew the victim* means she told you something. You could be called to testify."

"There's no reason for me to be called as a witness. All I did was sketch the guy who beat her up. Besides, anything I said would be hearsay, inadmissible."

"MS-13 doesn't necessarily understand that. They're in panic mode, nervous about what will happen with the trial now that the star witness is dead. They may think you're a loose end."

A loose end with the most dangerous gang in the states and her shop being used in a smuggling scheme. When had she lost control of her life?

Gus stroked a hand down her hair. "I'm with you until this is over."

The longing to be with him was creeping back and that was another issue. She wasn't sure whether that was good or bad. With a heavy, fatalistic sigh, Mary-Dee slipped from his grasp. "I'm going to inventory another box of Aunt Nellie's stuff. We need to put out new merchandise."

He went back to the sales counter where Kayley finished ringing up a customer. "Is Mary-Dee okay?" Kayley asked. "She seems tense."

"She will be. Dealing with a dead body shook her up."

"Surely, it wasn't the first time. She was an agent once." Kayley gave a questioning tilt of her head.

"Yeah, but that doesn't mean it's easy. It never gets easy." As he'd come to realize. The shop bell rang again. "I'll get this one."

Kayley stopped him with a hand on his shoulder. "No need. She comes in all the time. Rarely buys anything, just talks. Lonely. I'll help her."

Kayley was such an unlikely villain. Kindhearted. Friendly. Charitable. Genuinely so. Not usually the personality of a crook. Mary-Dee may be right. Kayley was being used by the smuggler.

Or she could be a very good actress.

Customer traffic slowed. Rather than sit behind the checkout desk, Gus went back to see if Mary-Dee had anything ready to be put out on the floor.

He stood in the doorway, watching her for a minute. Her shoulders slumped with the weight of the smuggling and the renewed threat from MS-13. She'd been through so much. Losing her Aunt Nellie, then Claudia. She didn't deserve all this. Guilt hammered at his conscience.

He tapped his knuckles on the doorframe. "It's slowed a bit. Can I help you?"

He picked up a turquoise cat figurine she'd finished inventorying. "I remember this. Still think it's giving me the evil eye."

"Someone will love it even if we don't." A smile lit her face.

He felt that tug again, the twist and pull.

CHAPTER TWENTY-THREE

AFTER THE SHOP closed, Mary-Dee and Gus drove to her farmhouse in companionable silence. Meena's Lincoln sat in front when they arrived. The sound of puppies yipping came from the backyard.

"What's she doing here? What if—"

Gus placed his hand on her arm. "No reason to get excited. The place is secure. I wouldn't have let her come if it wasn't safe."

"You told her she could come?"

"Not exactly. She sent a text saying she was bringing supper."

"Say no more. When Meena's made up her mind, there is no stopping her."

Lady, trailed by her six bouncy offspring, met them at the back door. "Well, hello there." Mary-Dee rubbed Lady behind her ears. "Good to see you and your family."

Gus squatted down to pick up a puppy. "I didn't know you were bringing Lady and the brood."

"She missed you and I couldn't very well leave the pups alone," Meena said.

Mary-Dee relaxed on the kitchen floor with the puppy kisses and playful pawing. Relaxed? As much as possible, knowing at any moment someone was going to break into her house to recover his smuggled goods. "It's nice to relax. We had oodles of traffic today."

"I'm sorry about the article. Eleanor had no business putting in all that detail." Meena sank into Aunt Nellie's rocking chair in a corner of the kitchen. The rocker gave a protesting creak.

"The good part is MDR had a banner sales day." *So there, Eleanor.*

When the first puppy curled up for a nap, Meena lifted the lasagna she'd brought into the microwave. "All talk of MS-13 and the newspaper article is hereby suspended. Eleanor will get her comeuppance, I promise you."

The meal finished and the dishwasher loaded, Mary-Dee led them to the den. Gus asked if Lady was allowed on the couch.

She nodded. Noticing the telltale sign of a puppy squatting, she picked the little guy up. "I'll take him out for a potty break."

Gus half-rose. She motioned him to stop. "No need. Security everywhere, remember."

"I'll join you just the same."

Meena followed and sat on the back porch. "These puppies are going to need forever homes soon," she said loud enough for Gus to hear.

"I'm working on it."

"We could put a flyer up at the shop," Mary-Dee offered.

Gus bent down to ruffle one of the puppies. "I can't give them to just anyone. I'd have to vet them first."

The puppies put on a show chasing one another. They all watched. After a bit, Meema came down the back stairs to gather a puppy in her arms. "It's time I got them back home. After all this excitement, they'll sleep well tonight."

Gus helped Mary-Dee gather the other pups into Meena's

car. The sun sank lower behind the barn as her Lincoln disappeared down the road.

Gus pivoted to the back door. His eyes locked on her. "The wait begins."

"You think he'll come tonight?"

"I don't know. I expect he's figured out where you live. So maybe."

She straightened her spine. "You want another coffee?"

"It's not a stakeout. We don't need to stay awake watching."

Mary-Dee gave a soft chuckle. "Like either of us is going to get any sleep tonight."

"Probably not. How about a movie? Something boring that will make us sleepy … unless you're ready to go to bed."

"I usually enter the sales slips into QuickBooks after supper." Humor lit his brown eyes.

"Before you say it," she went on, "I know I should get rid of the cash drawer and written tickets, automate everything, but I enjoy doing it the way Aunt Nellie did."

"You do that then." Gus went into the den and picked up the television remote. "I'll channel surf till you finish."

He flipped through the channels, paused on a history channel program about survivalists then moved on to *The Antiques Roadshow.*

The lure of descriptions that drifted across the room was too much. Mary-Dee shut down her computer. "You still watch this?"

"Meena says it's great for up-to-date pricing. That why you watch it too?"

"That and I learn so much." She nestled beside him. *Mistake.* The spicey scent of his aftershave circled her with memories of other times together on the same loveseat.

She tucked her leg beneath her and scooted into the corner for added distance. Which did nothing to slow the increased tempo of her heartbeat.

The outtakes of people who'd brought things for the experts

to price rolled on the screen with the credits. When those ended, she yawned. Not a made-up yawn, a real *I'm exhausted* expression of weariness that filled her to the bone. "It's still early, but I'm calling it a night."

"Good idea. You go on up. Maybe take one of those girly baths." Rising, he walked her to the stairs, closed his hand over hers on the circular newel post. "This will all be over soon. I'm going to double-check windows and doors then I'll be up."

The strongest urge to kiss him filled her. He'd spent the day, and evening, diverting her attention from the dangers that lurked. Meena's bringing supper and the puppies—all planned to keep her mind busy and occupied. She appreciated his efforts. Only appreciation wasn't all she felt.

She leaned in, to him, to that yearning and stopped herself. Better not to encourage this tingling she felt.

"I do feel safe," she said softly and ascended the stairs.

Bubbles rose in the clawfoot tub. The scent of lavender and roses filled the air. Mary-Dee slid down into the froth up to her chin. She must have dozed off because the click of the bedroom door across the hall woke her.

Gus was going to bed.

With her head on her pillow minutes later, she heard every creak and groan of the 19th-century farmhouse plus knowing Gus slept across the hall, sleep didn't come. Finally, she gave up and started downstairs for a cup of warm milk with a little Quik, her surefire sleeping aid.

If Gus yelled at her, he yelled. She patted her robe pocket. Her gun bounced against her hip. Let the smuggler come. This time she was ready.

At the bottom of the stairs, she halted.

A sound came from outside. A tremor ran up her back, urging her to turn around, go back upstairs, and wake Gus. She stopped with her foot mid- air. Hadn't she said over and over she could take care of herself?

This was her home. She'd protect it too.

Pivoting, she marched across the entryway and taking a deep breath, opened the door.

Gus checked the locks on all the doors and windows downstairs again. Rubbing his hand over the back of his neck where the tension concentrated, he headed up the stairs and checked all the bedroom windows except Mary-Dee's. He'd secured those earlier.

After a quick cold shower that did nothing to cool down his thoughts of her across the hall, he stretched out on the king-size bed and blanked his thoughts.

His eyes popped open minutes later. His mind and body awake in an instant. The luxury of drifting slowly awake had been given up years ago when he'd become an agent.

He'd perfected the ability to sleep quickly and lightly and to awake as quickly, ready to function. A habit he might have to forfeit if he was forced into early retirement.

Pulling on sweatpants, he didn't bother with shoes and went across the hall to check on Mary-Dee. Her door was open. He clamped his teeth. Stupid woman had gone back downstairs.

At the top of the stairs, he saw the front door wide open and her nowhere to be seen. His feet only hit two or three stairs on the way down.

"What the —" Gus barked as Mary-Dee rounded the corner of the house. "What are you doing?"

"Checking out something I heard."

"Alone? Why do you think I'm here? You should have awakened me."

She took a deep breath and counted to ten before she spoke.

"I'm prepared. Obviously, your *security* was not. Someone got through."

"Wait right here. I'm going to check the gate."

"I'm coming with you." she stepped into pace beside him.

When they found the FBI agent at the entrance gate, out cold, his head bleeding, she wished she had listened to Gus. She hated this part when she'd been an agent, liked it even less now.

Gus squatted down to examine him. The agent opened his eyes and raised his hand to his bloody head. "What happened?"

"That's what we want to know." Gus helped him stand. "Did you see who hit you?"

"Afraid not. I was checking the gate and next thing I knew I was on the ground."

Gus's eyes met hers then glanced back at the house. He'd left the door wide open. Mary-Dee nodded. "I'm on it. You take care of him." She sprinted down the driveway.

Gus hoisted the agent against his shoulder and wrapped a finger into his belt loop to hold him upright while he walked him inside.

Minutes later, Gus gave a questioning tilt of his head as he settled the agent on her couch.

"All's good," Mary-Dee answered. "The desk hasn't been tampered with." She checked the agent's injured head. "I'll clean this up ..."

"Jason," the agent filled in.

"We should probably call EMT. You could have a concussion." She dabbed at his temple with a tissue.

His face contorted. "I'd rather not."

"It looks deep, probably needs stitches."

"Let's decide after you've cleaned it." Jason's eyes pleaded.

"Fine." She disappeared upstairs for the First Aid kit.

Jason's made eye contact with Gus. "I'm on probation. This will be my third line-of-duty *accident*. I'd rather not make a big to-do, Sir." He dipped his chin to the floor.

"I understand." Gus appreciated the young recruit's predicament. "You didn't see anyone, hear anything."

"No, sir. I came to when you got there. We could check for footprints."

"Too many to single out a suspect – mine, Mary-Dee's, and yours. Relax. Once she's got you cleaned up maybe you'll remember something."

CHAPTER TWENTY-FOUR

WHILE MARY-DEE WENT upstairs for supplies, Gus checked the little drawer again. Still secure. No signs it had been tampered with. It didn't make sense. Smyth wouldn't knock out a guard, he'd kill him. Someone else or something else must have come. MS-13 back for another check on Mary-Dee?

"You sure you didn't see anything? A shape?" he asked Mary-Dee when she returned. Suspect sketching, she was an expert on physical characteristics.

"I only heard something. Never saw anything."

"Think. You too, Jason. There's bound to be some little detail." He rubbed his fingers up and down his forehead above his nose.

"Come look at this." Mary-Dee motioned Gus over and pointed to the cut on Jason's head.

"I see." Gus stepped around to face Jason. "Looks like you have tree bark in the wound. Do you remember hitting a tree?"

"All I remember is hearing a sound and whirling around to look. I didn't even pull my weapon." His eyes met Gus's. "Another mistake. But I didn't see anything. I hit the ground and came to with you standing over me."

"I'm going outside to look again. Where's your flashlight?" Gus asked Mary-Dee

"In the kitchen."

"Okay. I'll grab it after I get some shoes. It's been way too long since I ran around in your yard barefoot." He waved the flashlight as he walked out the front door moments later.

First, he checked the side of the house where Mary-Dee had heard sounds, he found what he suspected. Animal prints. Some obliterated by hers. A raccoon if he remembered his Boy Scout tracking correctly. And, from the size of the footprint, a very large raccoon. Smiling, he tracked the prints back toward the front gate then returned inside.

"Good news. Only fresh tracks I see are animal. A large raccoon. Large enough to have knocked you down, Jason."

Mary-Dee shook her head. "I charged out for a raccoon? I don't believe it."

Gus offered the flashlight. "Go see for yourself."

"I'm not questioning you. I just can't believe it. All the years I've lived out here … A raccoon—" She started to laugh.

Jason's shoulders relaxed. His chuckles joined hers.

Gus smiled. "Thank God we didn't call for backup."

Mary-Dee closed the First Aid kit. "I'll put this away. Who's for coffee? It'll be daylight soon."

"I'll start it." Gus headed to the kitchen, took the coffee tin from the cabinet, and poured grounds into the coffee maker.

"You live here?" Jason asked.

"Protection duty."

"Personal?"

"Yes and no. I'll tell you one day." His voice dropped off as Mary-Dee entered.

"Anyone for eggs? I can get some from the hen house," Mary-Dee offered.

"None for me. I'd best get back out there," Jason said.

"You?" she asked Gus when Jason disappeared out the back door.

"Let's sit on the porch and drink our coffee first."

They sat quietly listening to the sounds of the day waking up. The sun crept slowly over the field while beams of sunlight played between the branches of the trees. Birds chirped, joining the chicken coop sounds and the squeak of their rocking chairs.

"I'm glad last night was only a raccoon." Mary-Dee wrapped her hands around her mug and took a sip.

"What were you thinking dashing out there like that?"

"Do. Not. Start and ruin this lovely morning."

"Sorry." But he wasn't sorry. He'd died a thousand deaths when he saw the front door open.

Todd climbed the back porch steps. "No one answered in front. I figured you'd be back here. What happened last night?"

"Which version do you want? Mine or hers?"

"That's it. I'm going to get the eggs. Todd, you joining us for breakfast?"

At Todd's nod, Mary-Dee slammed her mug on the small table between the rockers and stomped down the stairs.

"Uh-oh. What'd you do this time? Another hunt cabinet moment?" Todd shook his head.

"No. Not this time. She heard a sound last night and charged out the front door. She was lucky. Poor Jason wasn't. A raccoon blindsided him."

"I think I'm going to need coffee for this one." Todd went inside. Gus followed for a refill.

Mary-Dee set the egg basket on the counter. Bending to the drawer below the oven, she jerked a skillet out. Pots and lids clattered and clanged. "Scrambled, okay?"

With the efficiency of a short-order cook, she fried bacon,

scrambled eggs, and filled a plate with toast. In between the cooking, she set the plates and silverware on the table along with homemade jam and butter. Once the eggs were done, she poured herself more coffee, sat, and filled her plate. "Any questions, Todd?"

Todd's cheeks dimpled as he tried to hold back the giggle, unsuccessfully. He covered his mouth. "Sorry. It's not funny. It could have been a nightmare. But that isn't why I came. There is good news about the gang members who attacked you two."

Mary-Dee gripped her fork on its way to her mouth.

Gus set his fork down.

"Both pled guilty to a Class 3 felony assault. The one with the gun serves concurrently with the firearm time. They'll be locked up for two years."

"That was fast," Gus said.

"Handled locally. Our new prosecutor is a barracuda. Threatened to add more charges. MS-13 lawyers backed down. The gang lawyers recognized the incarcerated pair strengthened their power inside. So all's good."

Mary-Dee took a deep breath. "What about Gianna's case?"

"D.C. lawyers are on it. No decision yet. He did say you wouldn't be calling you as a witness. Your testimony about anything Gianna said to you would be challenged as hearsay and thrown out. He's put in a request to move the trial to Alexandria. We're waiting on a decision."

"That pretty well settles Mary-Dee's issues with MS-13." Gus placed his knife and fork on his plate and carried it to the sink.

"But she still isn't in the clear. There's the little matter of the desk." Todd stood and set his plate on top of Gus's. "Which brings us to the other reason I'm here." He turned around, crossed his arms, and leaned his hip against the kitchen counter.

Gus interrupted him. "I got this. You're not going to MDR

today. Intel says Smyth will come for the diamonds today. I need to be here."

"I don't have to be here. I could go." Mary-Dee slammed her fork on the plate so hard she thought she'd cracked her favorite Fiesta plate.

"True. Nothing I'd like better than you away from the danger," Gus said.

Todd nodded. "But you'd be nervous and fidgety. Kayley would pick up immediately that something was going on. We can't have that."

As much as she didn't want to admit he was right, he was. Kayley would see right through her. "Fine. I'll get Meena to cover for me."

She'd figure out what to do with Gus all day long. Last night with him across the hall had been torture. All day...

Turned out the day sped past. She took care of MDR books and Gus helped her with little projects like changing light bulbs she couldn't reach.

Late afternoon, Meena called from the front door. "Company coming in." Lady and the puppies whipped around her, nearly buckling her knees. She grabbed at the doorframe. "We brought supper."

Mary-Dee glanced at Gus, mouthing, "You called her?"

"Not this time."

"Lady and the pups have been by themselves all day. They needed some company. Butch let them out once for me, but it wasn't enough. Being kenneled all day has them full of energy." Meena winked as she carried the casserole dish to the kitchen. "Made this before I left for the shop. Just needs to be heated up. We can play with the dogs while we wait."

"Let's put them out back so they can run." Gus herded the

six rambunctious puppies out the back door. Lady stayed with Mary-Dee.

Meena laughed. "She needs a break too."

"So how'd things go at the shop?" Mary-Dee asked.

"Gawkers mostly from reading the article. Solely disappointed you weren't there. We did sell a few things. The Duncan Phyfe breakfront went." Meena's cheeks rose in a clown grin. "I know you'll be glad that gigantic piece is gone."

"Thrilled." Mary-Dee had accepted the large dining room buffet-China cabinet from a friend. It'd been crowding the shop for months. She'd expected it to sell quicker. Now she could rearrange things. "Julie will be thrilled. How was Kayley?"

"Twenty-questioned me about you and Gus."

"I hope you told her nothing was going on."

Meena loaded the casserole in the oven. "Of course. But I can hope. Come on, Lady. Let's join the pups."

Mary-Dee rolled her eyes and followed her. Gus didn't call her the Energizer Cupid Bunny without reason. She was determined the two of them would get together. Had been since their teens.

After Meena and Lady plus her puppies were gone, Mary-Dee and Gus cleaned up the dishes, working in tandem, then settled in for a movie on television like a long-married couple.

Later at her bedroom door, they said goodnight. He gripped her upper arm lightly. "No going downstairs tonight. Do you understand? You hear something, you come get me."

His tone made her feel like a recalcitrant child. "I'm not six," she said between clenched teeth and closed the door in his face.

Gus blew out an exasperated sigh, started to cross the hall, and changed his mind. He tapped softly on the door. "Mary-Dee."

Nothing.

He tapped again. "Please."

He was about ready to give up when the doorknob twisted. She opened it enough for him to see her face. "What?"

"I'm sorry."

She studied his face, testing whether he was being honest. He pushed the door open more, cupped her chin, and kissed her forehead.

"Goodnight," he whispered and crossed the hall.

CHAPTER TWENTY-FIVE

THE FARMHOUSE WHISPERED and trembled like an old woman as Gus tried to fall asleep. Time dripped by minute by endless minute. Eric called earlier. Intel they'd intercepted confirmed the buyer had been given an ultimatum. Diamonds by the weekend or he was gone. Smyth, or whoever the smuggler was, had run out of time.

Gus folded his hands behind his head and listened for any sound. All he heard was Mary-Dee in her room tossing and turning the same as him.

At some point, he dozed off because he found himself jettisoning up. It took only a second to sort out that the sound came from downstairs. Wide awake, he slid out of bed and grabbed his gun. He'd slept in his clothes confident tonight would be the night. Careful to avoid the floorboard he knew creaked, he inched down the stairs with his back pressed to the parlor wall.

At the bottom of the stairs, he raised his gun and swung around into the parlor doorway.

Butch was at the cottage desk opening the drawer with the diamonds.

Gus's brain scrambled to wrap around the situation. His cousin, breaking and entering, searching for diamonds. Impossible. "Butch, what are you doing?"

"Getting stuff out of the desk."

"How'd you get in here?" Gus hadn't heard the alarm, and the door didn't appear to be forced open.

"Key under the flowerpot. Mary-Dee showed me and said I could let myself in anytime." He blinked his almond-shaped eyes.

"And the alarm?" Mary-Dee asked from behind Gus, her gun raised.

"Dad got the code at work." Butch hugged the drawer to his chest. "I was trying to be quiet."

"Sit down." Gus held out his hand. "Give me the drawer."

There was no way Butch was part of the international smuggling gang that Gus spent the last two years chasing. He was just doing what he'd been told. He had no idea who his parents worked for or any idea that what he was doing was illegal. Gus asked anyway, "Who are you working for?"

Butch dipped his chin and drew his lips into a pucker. "Mom. She wanted a bag out of the desk. But nothing's there."

Gus turned to Mary-Dee. "Call Todd. Tell him what's happened and to send a patrol car. No lights or sirens."

"But, Gus ..." Butch pleaded.

"No buts. You've royally messed up this time, cuz."

And so had Gus. He'd been too quick to dismiss his criminally inclined relatives. But then so had Todd. Stupid on both their parts.

Uncle Dwayne, and Aunt Darlene, spent their entire lives flirting on the edge of major crime. Looked like, this time they'd crossed the line and dragged their special needs son with them.

Gus pulled plastic gloves from his pocket. Prying the bottom from the false bottom loose. He removed a velvet bag. No need to look inside, he could feel the shape of the stones.

"Todd's on the way." Mary-Dee returned, her gun no longer visible, and reached for the bag.

He held it away from her. "DNA. Get me a food storage bag. I don't have an evidence bag."

"Gus," Butch began again.

"Sit." Gus pointed to the couch. He pulled the desk chair over, straddled it to sit in front of Butch. "Not a word until Todd gets here."

This takedown should have been a slam dunk. Nab the smuggler when he broke into Mary-Dee's. Easy. If only the smuggler had come instead of Butch. Gus had to find a way to salvage the operation and save Butch.

Todd arrived with Sam. "Take him to the station and put him in my office."

Sam motioned Butch from the couch. Gus followed them to the patrol car.

"I didn't do anything wrong," Butch pleaded.

"We'll figure this out," Gus reassured him and prayed he could protect his cousin. The last thing he wanted was Butch in jail.

Dwayne or Darlene deserved jail time. Unfortunately, once the smuggler learned they didn't have the diamonds jail might no longer be on the table. Smyth would not be happy. He'd probably shoot them.

Sam placed his hand on Butch's head as he slid into the backseat of the patrol car. Once the door shut, Sam turned back to Gus. "You don't think he's part of this?"

"Of course not."

"Me either." Sam climbed behind the wheel and drove away.

Gus called Eric to give him an update. "Yes, sir," he answered minutes later and slid his phone into his pocket.

Back inside, Gus found Todd and Mary-Dee talking in the parlor.

"I agree," Todd was saying.

"No way am I pressing charges against Butch. Dwayne and Darlene are the culprits." Mary-Dee looked at Gus.

"Butch didn't get to the diamonds. Nothing for feds to charge him with," Gus confirmed. "But Smyth's plan is blown. Failure isn't an option in an international smuggling operation. The criminal's communication network is as fast as Mount Pleasant gossip. Agents are on their way to the hook up place for Dwayne and Darlene."

"Let's pray they get there in time. They might be able to identify the smuggler," Mary-Dee said.

"I doubt it. Dwayne and Darlene probably don't have a name. Or the correct face."

"What are we going to do with the diamonds now?" Mary-Dee pointed to the black velvet bag in the quart food storage bag on her cottage desk. "There's got to be a way to salvage this operation." Frustration filled her words as she crossed her arms over her chest.

"Why don't you make us some coffee? We'll work on a plan."

Gus motioned Todd to the far corner of the parlor. "She doesn't need to be a part of this." He leaned in and explained Eric's plan.

Reappearing minutes later, she set the tray with three mugs on the trunk serving as her coffee table. "Why are you two huddled over there?"

Gus took his mug and sat on the couch. His gaze fixed on hers. "No reason."

Todd slipped his phone back in his pocket and declined the mug she offered. "I'm going back to the station. You know how everyone watches out for Butch. It'll just take one phone call to start the gossip train that Butch is in jail. My office will be overrun with people demanding he be released. I need to be there."

"We'll head to the shop like nothing's happened. He won't

risk doing anything in broad daylight," Gus said and prayed he was right.

"I don't like this." Mary-Dee hugged Todd.

"Neither do I. You and Gus be safe."

CHAPTER TWENTY-SIX

Gus and Mary-Dee headed to MDR, arriving well before opening time. She set out the doughnuts and made coffee. He placed the diamonds in the office safe.

"It's done." He joined her at the coffee station. "Everything hinges on Dwayne and Darlene doing what Todd told them to do."

Todd had contacted Dwayne and Darlene on their way to meet Smyth and told them to tell Smyth that Butch hadn't found the diamonds and Mary-Dee said they were in the MDR safe.

"What if they don't."

"They will if they want to survive. Smyth will not be a happy that they don't have the diamonds." He could kill them. Gus wasn't bringing that up.

"That's why using them to bait the smuggler doesn't set well with me. She gave her best narrow-eyed look. "We both know what it means —"

"Not now. Here comes Kayley. Don't give her any reason to sense something is up. Stay calm and collected. I know you can."

He leaned forward and placed a kiss, soft and featherlike on her lips. When she pulled away, he whispered, "For Kayley's benefit."

"You're back. Feelin' better?" Kayley picked up a doughnut for herself.

"Much. Thanks for handling things. Meena said the crowd of lookers thinned yesterday. I'm hoping today will be calm." Mary-Dee kept her face neutral.

"The notoriety will keep fresh faces coming. That's not all bad. Sales are up. I'll go turn on the sign and unlock the door. It's that time." Kayley sashayed to the door.

"I can't believe she's been working with smugglers, and I never suspected."

Gus pressed his finger to her lips in a shush sign. Mary-Dee frowned.

"I'll go work the desk with Kayley. You keep busy elsewhere. As tense as you are, she'll pick up on it."

———

By closing time, Mary-Dee's palms had permanent grooves from clenching her fingernails instead of confronting Kayley. She forced a smile as the woman gathered her purse to leave. "See you tomorrow."

Kayley hugged her. "I'm so glad the MS-13 mess has moved to Alexandria. Maybe you can relax a little ... until the trial. See you tomorrow.

"Kayley just gets to drive away?" Mary-Dee closed her eyes to shield her disbelief. How could Kayley even sleep knowing what she was doing?

Gus placed a gentle hand on her shoulder. "An agent is following her and there's one watching her apartment. Let's go."

"But I thought we were going to stay here with the diamonds."

"I am. You're going home. Where you'll be safe. This is Agent Caleb. He's going to take you then stay with you."

A man who looked enough like Gus to be his twin came toward her. Same height, and weight. Hair color and clothes. He extended his hand.

"Caleb."

She felt each joint in her spine go stiff. "Mary-Dee, and I'm not leaving."

Gus led her to the coffee station. A thin shell of hard slid over his face. "Yes, you are. I allowed Claudia to have her way, and it got her killed. That's not happening with you. You're leaving with Caleb. No arguments."

She looked into his eyes keenly aware she was on thin ice. Arguing would crack that ice. Realization sunk in with his words. Gus blamed himself for Claudia's foolish behavior that got her killed as much as if he'd fired the gun. If anything happened to her, he'd … she wasn't sure what he'd do but it would devastate him. She didn't want that.

"I'll go," she said quietly.

Gus exhaled the breath he'd been holding. "Thank you. I'll see you after this is over."

Mary-Dee walked with Caleb to Gus's truck. He opened her door. "He'll be fine."

"How can you be sure?"

Caleb didn't answer until he settled behind the wheel of Gus's truck. "This time he asked for help. Half your customers today were FBI agents." He put the truck in gear. "He's surrounded and we won't fail him this time."

———

Inside the shop, Gus settled in for a long night. Earlier, he used a clone of Kayley's burner to send a text to Smyth that the black bag was back at the shop. He hadn't received a response. Not that he expected one. It was more insurance in case Darlene and Dwayne didn't get their message delivered.

Timing was the unknown. Gus had no idea when, or if, Smyth met with his aunt and uncle. He texted Todd again to check on Butch. No response. That wasn't good.

All he could do was wait.

At the farm, Mary-Dee prepared supper. She'd nibbled doughnuts all day and wasn't hungry. Caleb, the young agent, hadn't. She tried Meena's number again as she stirred the spaghetti sauce. No answer and Meena always answered. That sent horrible scenarios through her head.

She wished she could go down to the covered bridge and sit on her log. Listening to the water lap would soothe the turmoil in her gut. It wouldn't be allowed. Instead, she buttered bread for garlic toast and when the oven timer dinged, she called her agent guard to supper.

After their meal, Caleb helped clean up. His mama would be proud. Then she went to her little desk and worked on entering shop receipts. Same as she'd done with Gus only days before. It seemed so much longer.

"Okay if I watch football?" Caleb asked.

"It's summer. I thought the season didn't open for a couple more months."

"Doesn't but old games are shown on the football channels. You have cable, don't you?"

"I do. Watch whatever you want."

Caleb scrolled until he found football game reruns and cheered as though it was a live-action game. Mary-Dee shook her head. He wasn't that much younger but a whole different generation.

She finished with the bookkeeping and excused herself. As

she settled into bed, she heard Caleb's cheers. His team must have won.

Sleep refused to come. Her thoughts centered on Gus alone at the shop. She pounded her fist into her pillow. She should have stayed with him.

The longer she stared at the ceiling the more urgent that need grew. She whipped back the covers. She had to be with him. Quietly she dressed and raised the bedroom window.

In her youth, she'd shimmied down the drainpipe to meet Gus. In the moonlight tonight, it looked rickety and a long way down to the ground. She closed the window and went downstairs.

"Caleb?"

"Something wrong?" He flipped off the television.

"There could be. I need to get to the shop. Where are my keys?"

"Ma'am, I don't think that's a good idea."

"I didn't ask. Where are my keys? They're supposed to be in this basket by the door."

"My guess, Gus has them. He gave me the keys to his truck."

"Fine. Give me those." She extended her hand.

"No can do." He rose.

Mary-Dee spotted the keys with his phone on the side table. She snatched them and dashed for the door. The next thing she knew, she was flat on her face on the ground.

"So sorry, ma'am. I can't let you do that." Caleb apologized as he pried the keys from her then lifted her to her feet. "Are you hurt?"

She responded by grabbing the keys from his hand, and holding them high, dashed to Gus's truck.

"Fine. I'm going with you." Caleb opened the passenger door before she got the truck into gear.

CHAPTER TWENTY-SEVEN

GUS TURNED OFF the shop lights and wandered through the shop looking out the plate glass windows. He settled in the office. Bored just sitting, he decided to go through Mary-Dee's receipts. He might get lucky and find sales for other furniture with stolen items. Mary-Dee did say Smyth was a regular customer on his trips through Mount Pleasant.

Sure enough, Gus located dozens of receipts over the last two years purchased by Smyth. Mary-Dee's sales transactions had details. Half of Kayley's sales only recorded the identity of the item, amount, and tax. A team would need to go through all her files thoroughly.

Summer daylight had faded when he finished the next year's receipts. He couldn't risk Smyth seeing light inside. He flipped off the light and positioned himself behind a large curio cabinet to wait.

An hour passed and no Smyth. He reached into his pocket to update Eric on what he'd found with the receipts when headlights flashed through the shop windows. A car pulled up outside.

Two figures got out and walked to the door. One, he pegged as Smyth and the other small frame probably a female. He confirmed it was Kayley when she used a key to unlock the door. The shop bell gave its cheery jingle. She went straight to the alarm box. Relocking the front door, they wended their way through displays to the office.

Gus drew his gun.

Speeding down the county backroad, Mary-Dee bounced on the truck seat and her foot rose above the gas pedal. Gus needed new shocks badly. She'd taken the longer route rather than the main roads to circle behind MDR hoping not to be seen. The poorly maintained roads made the ride all the bouncier.

She turned off the roadway into the field across the road from the shopping center. A gate blocked the entrance. With a head tilt to her passenger, Caleb hopped out and swung the gate open. She pulled the truck inside and slid out. They walked the last half mile to the shopping center.

Regret walked with her. This was all her fault. If she hadn't insisted on bringing the desk home, none of this would have happened. She was not going to let Gus be hurt for her whim.

Caleb tapped on her shoulder as they neared the line of businesses with her shop on the far end. She pointed forward and crouched against the buildings.

Beams of approaching headlights under the interstate turn-around blinded her. Caleb pushed her to the dirt as the car completed its turn. Mary-Dee swallowed and wiped dirt from her palm on her pants. Had to be the smuggler. None of the stores were open at this time of night.

She inched forward to the back door of MDR.

Caleb thumbed toward the door, asking if they were going in.

Mary-Dee shook her head and motioned to the corner. The back door opened into storage where layaway furniture was stacked. It would have been a good option. Only, Gus installed a bar across the door to prevent entry after he learned about the other break-in.

She rounded the corner of the building. Peeking through side windows to the front, she saw the dark-colored sedan with its headlights on.

Voices came from inside. Loud shouting. A gunshot. Then another.

She rounded the corner in a sprint and burst through the door to see Kayley face down on the floor. Blood pooling around her body.

Mary-Dee motioned for Caleb to look after her. She inched forward toward the office. From the doorway she saw Smyth had a gun pointed at Gus. She gripped her gun tightly to steady her hand shaking in rhythm with her pounding heart and stepped forward.

"You didn't need to shoot her. She did what you wanted."

"What an ex-FBI agent with no stomach for violence? She'd served her purpose." Smyth gave a wheezy chuckle. "Death is an occupational hazard in our business. Ask your boyfriend here."

"Not boyfriend. Agent." Gus corrected. "Game's up. You and your team have been under surveillance since Florida. You are the last to fall."

"I don't normally get this involved with shipments. But so many locals were so cooperative, and Ms. Ross here so charming. I couldn't resist." He shifted his eyes back to Gus. "I don't suppose either of you is the type to take a lucrative bribe."

"You suppose correctly," he answered.

Mary-Dee shook her head.

"That's too bad." Smyth lunged toward her knocking her

gun from her hand. His arm circled her throat. His gun pressed against her temple. "Put your gun down, *Agent*."

Gus hesitated.

Smyth smiled. "It is a small weapon compared to yours, but it works well at this range."

Gus let his gun drop. "Okay. Let her go."

"I don't think so. She's my insurance."

"Mr. Smyth." Her voice came out scratchy as she gripped the arm that constricted her airway.

"You keep choking her and you won't need a bullet."

"Right." Smyth loosened his hold. The gun remained pressed to her temple. Mary-Dee sucked in a breath. Smyth looked between them. "She is a lovely creature, isn't she? You wouldn't want her to end up like her sister, now would you?"

"Let me go and put the gun away. I'll go with you," Mary-Dee said in a weak ploy to buy time. The other agents and Todd had to be on the way.

"Oh, my dear, we all know that's not an option much as I'd like to for your sake. I so enjoyed our visits when I came to the shop."

"You'll never get out of this," Gus said.

"My escape routes are well plotted." He gave a devious smirk. "I always leave a back door open."

Mary-Dee's eyes shifted to meet Gus's. She strained to hear the sound of sirens. "Gus must have told you the FBI knows everything."

"Oh, yes, I knew. I may have miscalculated how close they were to the truth. I have the diamonds now and it's time to go."

"Are you sure the diamonds are in the bag? Did you look?" Mary-Dee grabbed his arm as it cut off her breath again.

Uncertainty clouded his face. Smyth jerked the gun from her head, shoved her to the side, and aimed it at Gus. "Move and I'll shoot him between the eyes. Don't test me. I'm an excellent shot. Ask that girl of yours."

Keeping his gun on Gus, he fished the velvet bag from his pocket, manipulated the drawstring open, and fingered the contents. He glanced down, and Mary-Dee made her move.

With every ounce of strength she had, she flung herself on Smyth's arm. The shot echoed in her head as she stumbled and was then shoved aside.

Her shoulder, on fire with pain, screamed as it connected with the floor. She landed in a heap. The coppery taste of blood filled her mouth as she scrambled up. Pushing her hair out of her eyes, she saw Gus's fist connect with Smyth's face.

The portly man staggered and headed for the back door. The last thing she saw before she fainted was Caleb in pursuit and Gus's face over her.

CHAPTER TWENTY-EIGHT

CONSCIOUSNESS RETURNED IN a blur of white fading to gray. Mary-Dee felt as though her body floated apart from her mind. Her chest and shoulder throbbed. As the cloudiness cleared, a white ceiling appeared and whatever dripped from the IV in her arm turned the white to gray then white again.

She shifted her gaze to the beige walls and the blinds raised to let in the sunshine. A pink plastic mug sat on the tray over her feet. Hospital, she squeezed her eyes shut. She truly hated hospitals.

Opening her eyes slowly, a person in a white coat leaned over her. "Doctor?" her voice came out whispery and made her frown.

"Miss Ross, how are you feeling?"

"Like I've been shot."

He chuckled at that as he took her pulse. "Good answer."

She moistened her dry lips. "How long have I been here?"

He aimed a slim flashlight at her right eye, then her left. "A few hours."

"It feels like days."

"Painkillers will do that. Hurting any place besides your chest and shoulder?"

Mary-Dee shook her head and immediately regretted the movement. "Where's Gus?"

"Pacing the hallway like a madman. He refused to sit in the waiting room with the others."

She lifted her head, letting it fall back again when the room whirled.

"Lie still," the doctor told her firmly.

"I don't like hospitals."

"A pity." He patted her hand. "You're going to be with us for a bit."

"Let me see Gus." Her eyelids threatened to droop. She forced them open. "Please."

"A few minutes only."

Gus leaned on the wall across from Mary-Dee's door. Thoughts and fears raced through his mind. She'd been unconscious on the ambulance ride. Better that way he rationalized. Made the pain bearable for her. But there'd been so much blood and her skin so pale.

Shock, it was shock he reassured himself. She'd be fine.

A headache pounded at his right temple. Why didn't the doctor come out? He'd been in there since she came from surgery. He'd give them five minutes more and then he was going in.

His stomach convulsed again. Swallowing, he forced his muscles to relax. His headache spread down the back of his neck. Fear turned to anger. He glared at the floor. He was going to burst through that door if they didn't let him see her soon.

The doctor appeared. "Gus?"

He grabbed the label of the doctor's white coat. "How is she? I want to see her now."

The doctor spoke calmly. "She's awake. The surgery went fine as I told you earlier. Why don't we sit down?"

His fingers tightened. "Why? What's wrong?"

The doctor took a deep breath. "Miss Ross is as well as can be expected."

"What does that mean? I want to see her."

"To answer your first question, she took a bullet, though a small one, it was at very close range and took its time exiting. You did an excellent job of first aid until the paramedics got there. Yes, you can see her in a moment."

Gus felt the blood drain to his toes. "An excellent job. What does that mean?"

"Exactly what I said. You did well. Does she have family?"

"There isn't anyone." Thanks to him. "Why?"

"We're gonna need to keep her in the hospital awhile. Then she'll need some help until her strength returns."

Gus stuck his hands in his pockets. A sense of helplessness covered him, sapping the strength that tension and anger had given him. "I'll take responsibility."

"What is your relationship to Miss Ross?"

He gave a short laugh. "It's long-standing and personal if that's what you're asking. Now I want to see her." He stepped around the doctor and pushed the door open slowly.

Shoving his hands back into his pockets, he crossed to her bed. A feeling of total inadequacy swept through him as his hands balled into fists inside his pockets. She was white as the sheets she lay on, and he'd done this to her.

Her eyes opened slowly. She lifted her hand to him. "I'm going to be fine."

He hesitated before taking it, gently squeezed. "I'm sorry."

"What for? You didn't shoot me." Her words were slurred from the morphine drip.

Her hand went limp in his. Her eyes closed again, and her breathing went deep before he could answer. "I shouldn't have involved you." He bent down and kissed her lips. "That's what I'm sorry for."

Back in the waiting room, he gave Todd and Meena the doctor's report. "I asked for some time before I have to go back to Quantico. Eric said he'd do what he could."

"Don't worry. We'll watch over her for you," Meena said and squeezed his hand. "She's gonna be fine."

Todd nodded in agreement. "Mary-Dee's strong. A bullet won't stop her. You got Smyth. That's what's important. His shooting Kayley was a major mistake. Attempted murder coupled with the smuggling charges means he's going down for a long time. He'll probably spill everything to reduce his sentence. You'll get the Europeans too."

"But I nearly lost another Ross in the process." Gus sank into the waiting room chair.

Todd sat beside him. "That's not the way it went down. Caleb was right outside the office. He said she lunged at Smyth. You had no control over that."

Meena sat on his other side and placed her hand on his knee. "Listen to Todd. This is not your fault any more than Claudia's falling in love with Smyth's son was."

He appreciated the support. Understood their words. Maybe in time he'd see it their way.

Gus sat at Mary-Dee's bedside as she regained her strength. The first couple of days she mostly slept. By the third day, her head began to clear, and she asked the one question he'd dreaded most.

"How is Kayley?"

Before he could answer the nurse arrived and settled her in the recliner by her bed. Her face blanched at the movement.

His expression neutral, he sat on the edge of the bed, giving her a chance to deal with the discomfort first. She didn't need to worry about Kayley or anything. She needed to focus on regaining her strength.

"Well? No one will give me an answer. I need to know."

He clenched his fists in the bed sheets and kept his voice controlled. "The bullet missed Kayley's spinal column. She has nerve damage, and it'll be a bit before she's very mobile."

"Will she be able to walk again?

"Doctors are hopeful."

"Has she explained how she got involved with Smyth?"

"We haven't been allowed to question her yet."

"I don't understand. Why did he shoot her?"

Gus's theory was Smyth was pulling out and cleaning up his mess. He would have killed both of us too if … he swallowed. "Theory is Smyth no longer needed her."

"I'll never understand how she could hook up with him in the first place."

"According to Smyth, she didn't know what she was doing for him."

"I don't believe him. She's smarter than that."

"But he's smooth. He fools people with his ability to become someone totally different with each of his disguised identities. That's why he's been so hard to pin down. No two descriptions matched."

Mary-Dee's eyes dipped to the floor. "He sure fooled me."

"You had no idea about the smuggling that had been going on. I couldn't tell you at first. If I had, you'd have connected the dots. That was your agent skill."

"I'd never wanted to need those skills after I left."

He moved over to sit on the arm of the recliner and kissed her head lightly. "I'm glad that you did – twice, or I'd be a dead man."

She tilted her head to look into his eyes. "I'm so glad I did too. I lo – "

His phone rang and the door opened, interrupting whatever Mary-Dee was going to say. The nurse carried a lunch tray. "You want to eat there or get back in bed?"

He motioned that he'd be outside answering his call. When he returned, Mary-Dee's smile dissolved into a pout. "You have to go, don't you?"

"I wish I didn't. Eric has been generous in letting me stay this long. I'll be back as soon as I can, I promise."

"Before you go, your aunt and Dwayne?"

"It was like Todd said, they saw an opportunity to pick up some cash. They had no idea what they'd gotten into. Fortunately, Dwayne got spooked when Smyth walked toward them. He knocked him down and ran back to the truck. Prosecutor's deciding how to charge them."

"Smyth let them go. Just like that?"

"There were a few bullet holes in Dwayne's truck and his leg, but otherwise they're both okay. By the time Todd's men got there, Smyth was already on his way to MDR."

"And Butch?"

"He won't be charged. While Darlene and Dwayne are in jail, he's hanging at Meena's helping with the puppies. We did find homes for two. Four more to go." He raised his hand with his fingers crossed.

Mary-Dee reached up and pulled his shirt, so his face was next to hers. "This. Was. Not. Your. Fault. Remember that."

Gus kissed her forehead. "I'll try."

CHAPTER TWENTY-NINE

AFTER A GRUELING debrief, tough talks, and tougher decisions, Gus returned to Mount Pleasant. He'd be called back to testify on occasion, but until then, no more agency. Smyth was his last bust.

His boss reluctantly signed off, promising to take him back any time he was ready. That would be never. After the last assignments of double living, lying to the people he loved, working undercover, and spanning the globe, he was ready for stability. Real roots.

He walked into Mary-Dee's hospital room to find her signing discharge papers. "You've been freed?"

"Finally. You're here." Her eyes shined. They hadn't when he'd left for Quantico. The weight on his heart lifted a little. He had so much to make up for.

"I hear you're staying with Meena."

"I can't convince anyone I'll be fine at the farm sleeping downstairs for a while."

"I agree with the majority.

The nurse arrived and assisted Mary-Dee into a wheelchair. Gus spotted the winces from the movement that she tried to disguise. At his truck, he tossed her suitcase into the truck bed and slid his arms beneath her knees to lift her into the passenger seat.

Still too thin. Meena's cooking would take care of that. Helping him with Lady and the remaining pups would put the color back into her cheeks.

"You didn't bring the SUV."

"Belongs to the Agency."

"I didn't think about that." A frown clouded her forehead.

Gus patted the steering wheel like he would Lady. "This has done me good. It's all the transportation I need."

As the truck approached the parking lot speed bump, Mary-Dee gripped the door armrest then relaxed as the truck glided over. "You got new shocks."

"Couldn't have you bouncing the way Caleb claims he did that night."

"Thank you. I do appreciate it. I don't feel much like bouncing today. How long do we have before you leave again?"

"About that … I won't be leaving. I resigned." He gave her a side-glance waiting for her reaction.

Her head whipped around toward him. "You what?"

"By mutual agreement."

A brittle silence like ice cords settled through the truck until he made the turnoff at the covered bridge. He pulled off the road, parked under the big oak tree and stared out at the Shenandoah.

"I'm ready, Mary-Dee. I should have taken the medical exit they offered after Claudia. I considered it until Smyth resurfaced here in Mount Pleasant. I had to be in on this operation the second I knew MDR was involved." He paused, rested his chin on the steering wheel. "I wanted to be sure you were protected and didn't do a very good job of that."

She reached over to turn his face until he was looking at her, not the river. "You did take care of me. I'm the one who got myself shot. I was petrified he was going to shoot you. I had to stop him. That's why I lunged for his gun."

"It was dumb. Caleb had my six."

"I'd told him to stay with Kayley."

"Agents don't always follow directions." A slow grin lifted his cheeks. "Let's get you settled at Meena's." He shifted into reverse and backed onto the road.

Meena met the truck in full mother-hen mode. "Gus, get her bag and take it to the back bedroom. I'll get her settled on the porch. She looks like she could use a cup of herbal tea and one of my scones."

"That would be heavenly." Mary-Dee settled at the table on the back porch where she and Meena had shared so many conversations over tea and scones. She was grateful that their days of playing the blame game were over and Smyth was behind bars. If only the MS-13 gang members who shot Gianna would be caught, her life could move forward again.

Mary-Dee took a deep breath of air free of hospital smells. Smiled and took another. "It's heavenly out here this time of year, isn't it? The heat and humidity will soon be gone. Summer is slipping to an end. You can feel the hint of fall in the air." Meena set the tray with a plate piled high with scones and three teacups on the table. "My favorite time of year."

"I'm just so grateful there are no hospital smells or noise. I'll live with heat and humidity. I hope you don't expect me to eat all of those."

"You won't have to. Gus and Butch will eat what you don't."

"Where is Butch?"

"He's over at the barndominium playing with the last puppy. New people are coming for a look today."

"You didn't tell me." Gus pulled out the chair next to Mary-Dee.

"Just happened this morning. They saw the sign on the door at MDR and called. That'll leave you with Lady. Adult dogs are much harder to find new homes for, you know." Meena gave Mary-Dee a conspiratorial wink. "I think you should keep her."

"Maybe. Don't know. She has grown on me," he said.

He'd keep Lady, Mary-Dee thought but didn't say. She'd watched him with the dog he clearly loved. "Every man needs a dog in his life."

"Point taken. I'm going to grab a few of these scones and go wait for the couple with Butch. If they take the pup, Lady will need comfort." He gathered all but two of the scones in a cloth napkin and went to his barndominium.

"He's gonna keep her," Meena said with a smug smile.

Mary-Dee nodded. "Did you know he's left the Agency?"

"I didn't know he'd actually resigned. He and Todd talked about it, but I didn't think he'd made a final decision."

"That's what he said. Is he thinking about joining the Mount Pleasant police?"

"That's a conversation you need to have with him. All he's said is he's going to help you get MDR back up and running once it's been released as a crime scene." She studied Mary-Dee over the rim of her teacup. "Have you thought about that?"

"Lots. I'm not going to let this ruin what I love. I'll need to hire someone else to replace Kayley, but I will reopen."

Meena reached over and patted her hand. "That's my girl. You're looking peaked. It's been a tiring morning. Why don't you go rest a bit?"

"I think I will." She pushed from the table after one last sip of tea and made her way to the back bedroom.

Gus rested his hand on Lady's neck as Butch helped the

couple load the last puppy. He cleared his throat. "It's just you and me now, girl."

And maybe one day Mary-Dee.

Todd's black police sedan pulled up. "All the puppies gone now?"

Butch answered, "Gus is going to be lonely without Lady and her pups."

"I'll be just fine, Butch."

"I think he's going to enjoy the peace and quiet," Todd said. "Gus and I need to talk. Can you go check on Meena and Mary-Dee?"

"Here take this back to her." Gus passed the hobo-knotted napkin to him.

"Wait, are those Meena's sconces? I'll take one." Todd untied the knot removed a scone then handed the rest back to Butch.

Gus grabbed one too. Butch headed toward the house munching on another.

A knot formed in Gus's stomach as he led Todd and Lady inside. "What's up?"

"Nothing bad." Todd sat at the counter while Gus fixed coffee. "I talked with the Commissioner. He's ready to make you an offer."

"I told you I'm not doing anything until Mary-Dee is back up and running."

"That's the other good news. The crime scene crew has finished. She can open as soon as she's strong enough."

Gus unplugged the coffeemaker and grabbed his keys. "Let's go check it out. Load up, Lady."

The dog was at the door before Gus. He looked back at Todd. "You can come too."

Gus used the key Mary-Dee gave him to open the door. He took a deep breath as the shop bell tingled above his head. Everything looked the same as it had before. He pushed the image of Kayley away and walked back to Mary-Dee's office. He froze in the doorway. A lump formed in his throat as the scene from that night raced through his head. Terror raced through him seeing again Smyth holding Mary-Dee at gunpoint, the deafening bullet, her body lying in a pool of blood, white and unconscious — her blood on his hands from trying to stanch the flow.

Guilt washed over him again.

"Don't do that." Todd's hand rested on his shoulder. "You wrapped this case up tightly. The domino theory is working well. One name's leading to another. We'll likely shut the whole operation down, and we have more than enough to put Smyth away. We won't have to worry about him for quite some time."

"At what cost?"

"Don't do that. You'll weather the aftermath and rebuild. So will Mary-Dee. Time to put it behind you and move ahead. The future awaits."

Todd was right. Dwelling on a case or the past got you nowhere. Gus swiveled to face the shop. "The memories will fade and, perhaps, the notoriety will help the business." Eleanor's reporting about Gianna's body at the book club had proved that.

"Until some other piece of news replaces it. What do we need to do here?"

"Not much. I'm impressed with your cleanup company. Looks like nothing except dust on everything. No rearranging. Mary-Dee will have to decide how she wants things displayed. We'll need to help with that until she can hire someone."

"What about Butch?"

"I was thinking the same thing. We'll see what Mary-Dee thinks after we have the place ready for her." Gus pitched a feather duster to Todd.

A week later, warmth seeped into Mary-Dee's chest and spread like a high tide through her veins with each rhythmic pulse when she walked into MDR with Gus and Lady. Not the anxiety she expected.

The storefront windows glistened. So did the glass display cases. All the furniture pieces glowed. It felt like the first day she'd opened. Except in her head visions of that night flickered. She shook them away. "Everything looks shiny and clean."

Gus raised his arm in a Rosie the Riveter pose. "I did it. Well, Todd and I."

"Me too. I helped." Butch followed them in the door.

"Yes, he did. A joint effort." Gus high-fived Butch.

"Thank you all."

Mary-Dee wouldn't allow her eyes to look down at where Kayley had lain. She went straight to the check-out counter. She couldn't face the office yet either, so she stuffed her purse in the bookcase behind the sales counter. Her fears that no one would come disappeared as three cars parked in front of the shop. With a deep breath, she went to the door to greet the customers.

By noon, she needed a nap which she wouldn't get because the customers kept coming. The ones rude enough to want details, she graciously passed on to Gus. The others she and Butch handled.

At the end of the day, all three of them were exhausted. When the antique grandfather clock chimed five p.m., Butch locked the front door and flipped the open sign to closed. "We did it!"

"We sure did."

The cookies Meena sent were gone though Mary-Dee feared Butch and Gus may have eaten a good many of them. She lifted the two-inch stack of sale receipts from her vintage cash box. Probably one of her best sales days ever. She'd be busy tonight.

Gus slipped his arm around her waist and pulled her close. "Yes, we did!"

She leaned into him and took a deep breath. "Thanks to you and Butch for all the help. You may need to ask your new boss for another day off to help if the crowds keep up."

"Todd wouldn't object, but you'll do fine with Butch and Lady."

Mary-Dee had been nervous about having a dog in the shop. Some customers don't like dogs, but Lady seemed to sense the ones who didn't and climbed into her bed behind the counter when they came in. She bent down and ruffled Lady's head. "You did a great job too."

"Do I need to do something before I go home?" Butch looked as tired as Mary-Dee felt.

"All good. See you tomorrow."

Gus locked the door behind him. "You need to do anything else?"

"Nope. It can wait until tomorrow. I'm exhausted."

"Let's get you home." He slapped his thigh and Lady came running.

Mary-Dee climbed into his truck with Lady settled between them on the seat. Country music filled the cab as they drove to the farm.

The day turned out much better than she had expected. She'd even gone into her office several times without flashbacks. "It's all over," she whispered to herself.

Lady nestled her head in her lap as they crossed the covered bridge and headed to her farmhouse.

After dinner, she input the sales receipts into her computer program, and Gus surfed TV channels with Lady settled next to him. When she finished, she walked over, cupped his cheeks, and kissed him. "Today's sales beat opening day. Thank you."

He tumbled her into his lap. "We make a good team. When are you going to marry me?"

She stiffened her spine. Had she heard correctly? Marriage to Gus had been her teenage dream. So much had happened she'd almost abandoned the hope. "Is that a proposal?"

"It is. What say you?"

"I don't deny I've thought about it, but there're a couple questions you need to answer first."

"What? I'll do or say anything you want."

"You and Lady will need to move in here."

"No problem. And?"

Lady thumped her tail as if agreeing.

"We move the hunt cabinet here into the dining room."

His head dropped back in a knee-slapping laugh. "Of course. I bought the thing for you. You're the one who didn't want it."

"At that point, I wasn't sure I trusted you. It seemed like a bribe," Mary-Dee admitted.

"And you trust me now?"

"I do. With my body, soul, and spirit, I love you, Gus Nolan. Always have."

CHAPTER THIRTY

Two years later

MARY-DEE ADDED ANOTHER newspaper article to the growing stack about the arrest and trial of the MS-13 gang members accused of Gianna's murder. The clippings grew daily since the story coverage was front page news in all the area newspapers.

Though she didn't know Gianna Paz personally, her brief contact brought a connection she still couldn't explain. The newspaper articles helped piece together the teenager's story. A profile Mary-Dee had learned as an agent fit too many young gang members. Alone in a country that didn't speak her language, Gianna found a family with the three-dot MS-13 tattoo and pretended the violence didn't exist.

She learned more details of Gianna's life from Honduras to San Franciso to Texas to Northeastern Virginia from her court-appointed guardian. No one knew for sure why she decided to turn informant except she'd seen one too many brutal murders and wanted to keep her unborn child safe.

Mary-Dee glanced down at her swelling belly and understood.

Isolation in safe houses and witness protection proved too hard on Gianna and that was what brought her to the banks of the Shenandoah the day of their book club.

Authorities worked for over a year to arrest and indict the four MS-13 gang members responsible. Between Gus's contacts and Todd's, they'd kept up with the process. Recently, a judge had declared the four arrested eligible for the death penalty.

Trial went to jury today. Gus and Todd had gone to Alexandria to be in court when the verdict came.

Mary-Dee could have gone. Her hands circled her swollen belly. She'd decided hearing the news long distance would be adequate.

She finished her coffee, rinsed her cup, and called Lady. "Load up. We're going to the shop.

Shortly after Mary-Dee and Lady arrived, the shop bell chimed. Lady's tail wagged as Meena walked through the door swinging a basket. "Cookies."

"Yay!" Butch trailed her to the coffee bar.

Mary-Dee joined them. "You didn't have to bring them in person. I could have sent Butch. It's kinda slow today."

"Nope. Not today." Meena shook her head. "We need to hear the news together."

A short time later, Mary-Dee's cell rang. Gus. She held her breath and put the phone on speaker.

"Two guilty on all counts. The one who planned it from his prison cell was acquitted along with a fourth man. Sentencing begins Monday." His voice twined with relief and disappointment.

Meena and Butch clapped in the background.

"I'm so glad, but disappointed two got off."

"They didn't exactly get off. Paz's boyfriend is already serving a life sentence so the not guilty means little. The other not guilty is also in jail on immigration detention. The convicted two will start appeals. I don't think they'll be effective. Just a lengthy process out of our control."

"That's the hard part." Mary-Dee sighed.

"We'll get through. Smyth's behind bars and his cohorts are falling like flies. Time to get on with our lives. I love you. See you soon."

"I love you too." Mary-Dee ended the call.

"It's over. Y'all come to the house when he gets back. I put chicken and dumplings in the crock pot before I came to the shop."

"Me too?" Butch asked.

"You and Todd both. We'll have a party," Meena answered. "A celebration that it's finally over." Meena slid her arm across Mary-Dee's shoulder and tucked her in a tight squeeze. "The new beginning for you and Gus."

She smiled down at her belly. "We'll all be able to move on with the rest of our lives."

AUTHOR'S NOTE

Dear Reader,

Dead Body Girl is based on a real-life event. In 2003, during a garden party at the home of family friends Ambassador James Nolan, Jr, and Mary B. Nolan, a dead body was discovered on the bank of the Shenandoah below their home. Mary B. and Jim suggested I write a story about what happened and willingly shared details and plot ideas. It has taken a long time for this finished product and sadly Jim and Mary B. are no longer with us. You'll see Mary B. in Mary-Dee and Gus is a fictionalized version of FBI agent Jim.

Thank you so much for reading Gus and Mary-Dee's story. Please consider leaving a review.

On the fence about leaving a review? It's okay to leave a star rating and say nothing at all.

Sharing about the book to friends, readers' groups, and social media will also help other readers find Dead Body Girl.

If you'd like to make sure you never miss a new release, sign up for my newsletter on my website, https://judythemorgan.com/

Until next time!
Judythe

ACKNOWLEDGMENTS

Ambassador James Nolan, Jr, and Mary B. Nolan - without whom this book would not exist.

Kay Vaccaro who shared plotting ideas.

Tess St. John for eagle-eye copy editing.

My husband, my cheerleader, my first editor/proofreader and always model for the hero.

My deepest thanks to you all. Without you, this book would never have been written.

ABOUT JUDYTHE

Judythe Morgan is a multi-published author who's been writing award-winning fiction since 2003. She believes novels should give you a break from real life and leave you feeling happy. You'll find strong characters mingled with a touch of mystery and suspense in her books, but no explicit content.

She lives in a small town north of Houston with her husband and Old English Sheepdog, Finnegan MacCool. She has three grown children, eleven grandchildren, three great-grandchildren, and nine granddogs who fill her life with fun and laughter. You'll find her on the porch swing with a glass of sweet tea and a book when she's not at the keyboard.

Follow Judythe on :
Facebook
Amazon Author Page
BookBub
Goodreads

OTHER TITLES BY JUDYTHE

Seeing Clearly
Thrilling suspense and seasoned romance

Consumed by grief and vengeance, Dawson McKey is on a relentless quest after a cartel's bomb takes the lives of his twin sons. He trusts no one and closes his heart to the possibility of love… until he meets overly trusting Evie Parker.

She's a widow raising her grandson after her only child and his wife die in a suspicious car accident. Overwhelmed and convinced their age difference would haunt a relationship, she resists their attraction.

When her grandson mysteriously vanishes, their lives become entangled in a dangerous race against time that tests their trust and budding love. Will they see clearly enough to find the toddler and each other?

Claiming Annie's Heart
An Irish Love Story

Annie Foster stays in Ireland after boarding school to nanny a widower's infant daughter. Five years later, the widower proposes.

Her first love Chad Jones, whom she believes abandoned her, arrives weeks before the wedding on an undercover assignment probing her fiancé's connection with IRA terrorists. Chad's determined to change Annie's mind and her heart because he's never stopped loving her.

Which man will claim Annie's heart?

The Promise Series

Two men and one woman met at Eighth Army Headquarters, South Korea in the turbulent Vietnam War years and their lives are irreversibly linked. The promises they made to themselves and each other bind their hearts forever.

The Fitzpatrick Family Series
Six siblings of a small-town minister find love and happily ever after.

Christmas Prom Rerun
A Small-Town Holiday Reunion Romance

Broke and divorced, Shannon O'Leary returns home to a teaching job at the high school she once attended. Tyler Evans, the high school sweetheart she jilted, never left. He's now a world-famous artist. Working together on the annual Christmas Prom decorations proves a challenging walk down Memory Lane. How can she put her life together again when her heart insists on falling in love with him all over again?

www.ingramcontent.com/pod-product-compliance
Lightning Source LLC
Chambersburg PA
CBHW071240130626

46556CB00003B/1102